TOUCH OF THE PAST

TOUCH OF THE PAST

JON L. BREEN

WALKER AND COMPANY
NEW YORK

First published in the United States of America in 1988 by
the Walker Publishing Company, Inc.

Published simultaneously in Canada by Thomas Allen &
Son Canada, Limited, Markham, Ontario.

Library of Congress Cataloging-in-Publication Data

Breen, Jon L., 1943–
    Touch of the past.

    I. Title.
PS3552.R3644T6   1988   813'.54
88-17134   ISBN 0-8027-5704-9

Printed in the United States of America.
10 9 8 7 6 5 4 3 2 1

For Margaret Breen
and in memory of Bill Breen,
married February 24, 1937

AUTHOR'S NOTE: Idyllwild is a real town, and some of its landmarks and institutions are mentioned by name in this book. However, none of the characters is based on an actual person, in or out of Idyllwild.

PROLOGUE

1937

THE HOST WAS a minor producer, one of the princes of Poverty Row, and of all the New Year's Eve parties in Hollywood, this one had to rank in the second hundred. There was a live band, though. Tonight every musician in the world must be working. Just the big band remotes on the radio, all over the dial, must involve thousands of them. All those horns, all those drums, all those snappily jerking batons. And all those guys listening to them, swinging to them, who had their girls in their arms.

The youngish man in the striped tie had found a comfortably obscure corner of the big room for some serious drinking, away from the band and the cheerfulness that seemed such an affront to one who was not feeling too ebullient. But the bores kept finding him.

"Hasn't it been a year?" the current bore was saying.

How could one reply? No room for disagreement, of course. By any standard, 1937 had indisputably been a year. For him, a happy year, an eventful year, but a year of unfinished business as well. He said none of that. Compulsively polite, he just said, "Sure has."

"Did you read E.V. Durling in the *Times* this morning?"

"Haven't seen it, no."

"Great a year as it's been for pictures, with studios turning profits as high as seventeen million dollars, how many studios do you think gave their employees a Christmas bonus?"

"Not the one I work for."

"Me, too, neither. But how many do you think?"

1

"Couldn't say."

"One, that's how many."

"Did he say which one?"

The bore shrugged. "Who do you like in the Rose Bowl game tomorrow?"

"Who's playing?"

"Come on, kiddo, you're not that drunk."

"I'm working on it."

"Me, I have to like Cal."

"Does that mean I have to like Alabama?"

"Only if you want a bet, and I don't want a bet. I spent too much money for Christmas. We went all out for the kids this year, all out. And the wife's relatives are all out, too."

The youngish man took a last swallow of his drink and started looking for a waiter to replenish it for him. He sensed the man opposite him expected some kind of response, and he had lost the train of the conversation. So he just said, "How's that?"

"All out from Nebraska." The guy laughed as if that was the greatest punch line he'd ever heard—the youngish man thought he'd have to hear the beginning of the joke some time. "I got a nephew marching in the Rose Parade tomorrow. Tuba player. The wife expects us all to troop over to Pasadena to watch it in the morning. And the relatives all know I did a picture with Leo Carrillo, who's the Grand Marshal. I have a feeling they're expecting to be introduced to him. With a million people lining the streets, they think I'll be able to introduce them to the Grand Marshal. I'm not looking forward to tomorrow, kiddo."

"You need your rest."

"I need another drink."

The waiter came to accommodate both of them, and the bore bore on. "I'd rather be going to Santa Anita. Seabiscuit was supposed to run tomorrow, you know, but the owner said the weight was too much. A hundred and thirty-two. That's not so much. You know what kind of weight they used to pile

2

on Discovery."

The man was talking gibberish. Just nod politely.

"Hey, you got a phone call!" The youngish man saw his host beckoning to him from across the room. Excusing himself gratefully, he got to his feet, took a surprisingly unsteady step, gained control of himself, and strode over with the iron dignity peculiar to the slightly drunk. In a hallway off the big room, he was handed the phone.

"Hello," he said doubtfully.

"Happy New Year, darling!" said the voice he loved more than any sound in the world.

"Hi there. Happy New Year. But it's only . . ."

"A little after nine o'clock where you are, but this is New York. I'm speaking to you from 1938, darling. Our year."

"Sure, I hope so." It was noisy where she was, and she sounded very cheerful. He didn't think he could match it.

"How's Larry's party?"

"Oh, real nice. Or it would be if you were here."

"You're not feeling sorry for yourself, are you?"

"What are holidays for? Christmas was worse."

"I'm missing you like crazy, darling, but pretty soon we'll be together forever and always and we'll be happier than any two people have ever been."

"I know we will. How's the show going?"

"I think we have a hit. The audiences are loving it. We may play for a year."

"Great." He couldn't keep the letdown out of his voice.

"Don't sound that way! It's an important play, and you should be able to find plenty of excuses to come to New York."

"I'll manage somehow, but it's a long way."

"Darling, you enjoy yourself tomorrow. Have a happy, happy New Year. What are you planning to do?"

"Work. I have to finish . . ."

"Oh, come on!"

"Well, if my hangover isn't too bad."

3

"Work well then. Give my best to Larry. And Monte if you see him. Somebody else wants to use this phone, so . . ."

"Where are you?"

"The greatest place in the world to be on New Year's Eve, darling. Except wherever you are, of course. I really have to go. Love you, darling."

"Love you," he echoed and hung up the receiver, feeling kind of numbed. He knew he was a happy and lucky man, but that didn't make this occasion any less lonely. Nothing for it but to have something more to drink.

He thought he'd found a new corner, but before he knew it, the same bore was back with him. "Lot of parties tonight. Best New Year's since before the crash, they say. The one *I'd* go to if I had the choice—or the invitation—is the one Stu Erwin and his wife are throwing."

"Uh, why's that?"

"Well, get this, it *starts* a minute after midnight at the Jimmy Gleasons' house. It goes all night, and all the guests wind up at the track tomorrow afternoon as the guests of the Erwins. Half the top comics in town are invited—Hugh Herbert, Victor Moore, Jack Benny, Andy Devine, Eddie Bergen—don't know if he's bringing the dummy with him or not, but it should be a riot. That's where I'd like to be tomorrow, not watching the Rose Parade with half the state of Nebraska. Don't get me wrong. I got nothing against flowers, but there's flowers all over the place . . ."

The monologue was starting to have little interruptions in it, like a bad radio transmission. For a while, the youngish man tried to make a pretense of staying in the conversation.

"He did?"

"Huh?"

"Who did what?"

"I'm telling you He Did. The horse to beat with Seabiscuit out of it."

"Oh . . ."

But pretty soon he and his striped tie were sprawled out

4

asleep on the couch. He'd drunk too much, too fast, but Larry wouldn't mind.

He had a faint impression of extra noise at the hour of midnight, but he offered no shouts or kisses, quickly returning to snores as the party noise returned to a steady drone.

It must have been hours later when he began to wake up, realizing some considerate soul had thrown a blanket over him, realizing the party was over, realizing he was in for one terrific hangover. And voices were speaking, faintly, at the edge of the room.

"The poor bastard."

"I know."

"How in the hell can we ever tell him?"

1

1987

HE WAS ONE of the most irritating people ever to walk through the doors of Vermilion's Bookshop. He was around the half-century mark but resisting it, with close-cropped grey hair and a pencil-thin mustache. He was selling rather than buying and in fact had the slick, overdressed appearance of a purveyor of dubious merchandise.

He was holding a dust-jacketed copy of Jack Finney's 1970 novel *Time and Again.* "This author is really collectible now, isn't he?"

"Oh, yes," said Rachel Hennings. "He's a wonderful writer."

"This is the first edition and I'd call this fine condition, wouldn't you?"

"I think so. May I have a look at it?"

"I know I could make more if I sold it to a private collector myself, but selling it to you saves me the bother and does us both some good, right? How much can you offer me? I'll take any fair price."

"May I have a look at it first?"

"Of course, I won't tell you what *I* paid for it. But you can find some real treasures at thrift shops and library sales if you keep your eyes open, can't you?"

"You certainly can. Do you mind if I look at the book?"

The customer handed it over with the care due a fragile and priceless heirloom.

Rachel looked at the front jacket flap, studied the title page and verso, took off the jacket to look at the binding, restored the jacket, and said, "I can only offer you two dollars, I'm afraid. This isn't a first edition."

The customer looked her in the eye as if she were insane. "But it *is* the first edition. I know it is."

There was something about him that rubbed Rachel the wrong way, but she did her best to remain pleasant. "I'm sorry, it's not. You see—"

"Look, right there," he said, poking at the verso of the title page with a long index finger. "See? It says 'first printing.' "

Rachel Hennings shook her head. "I see what it says, but it's *not* the first edition."

"Oh yeah, then why does it say it is?"

"I don't know why, but it's the Book-of-theMonth-Club edition."

"Well, isn't the Book-of-the-Month-Club edition the same as a first edition?"

"No."

"But it *can* be the same."

"No, it can't."

The customer looked at the book again, as if reconfirming the evidence of his senses. "No, you're wrong," he insisted. "Look. It says on the dust jacket it's a Book-of-the-Month-Club *selection*, yes, but there's also a price on the jacket. That means it was sold through a store, not through the mail."

Telling herself it was a fine point, something he didn't necessarily know, and that he probably wasn't intentionally trying to cheat her, Rachel maintained her civility, saying, "Let me show you something."

She took the book from the customer's hands, removed the jacket again and pointed to a small indentation in the bottom right corner of the book's back cover. "See that? That means it's the Book-of-the-Month-Club edition. They always have that little blind stamp there. My uncle taught me that the first summer I worked in this shop. This is not the first edition, and I can't pay you a first edition price for it. It's a good reading copy, though, and I think two dollars is more than fair."

The customer pouted like a baby deprived of his rattle. "And how much will you sell it for?"

"I might price it at four or five dollars. And I'd probably sell it for that eventually, but I can't be certain of when."

"Listen, baby, I've seen the first edition of this book listed in catalogs at a hundred bucks."

"I'm sure you have, but this isn't the first edition."

"Well, I'm going to take this book to somebody who knows his business." He stomped to the front of the shop and said to a tall, elderly browser, "You said she knew her stuff."

The older man looked amused. "She's always seemed to."

"Not this time. Thanks for the ride, Gil. I'll see you back on the hill." He threw a last pitying glare at Rachel and stomped out of the shop, slamming the door behind him.

Rachel sighed. The book business had been good to her. She'd enjoyed it in the couple of years since she'd taken over her late uncle Oscar Vermilion's shop, but in any business there were headaches and that hothead had been one of them. Surprisingly enough, he'd come into the store with one of her favorite customers, Gil Franklin, who was looking both tickled and apologetic now.

"Is that guy a friend of yours, Gil?"

"Not exactly, but he bummed a ride down from Idyllwild. Doesn't need one back, and I can't say I'll miss his company."

"Who is he?"

"Jud Crompton. He's a real-estate salesman up there."

"Real-estate salesman? How does he sell anything to anybody with that short fuse?"

"Oh, he's not such a bad guy. He only gets mad if you don't agree that he's a leading expert in any field you can name."

"I sure hope he knows more about houses than he does about books."

"A little bit, I guess. Sorry to inflict him on you. If I spend a lot of money will you forgive me?"

8

Rachel smiled and shook her head. "Nothing to forgive, Gil. And I won't let him sour me on *Time and Again*. It's one of my favorite books. How was the drive down from the hill?"

"Terrible. Besides having to listen to Crompton, I got behind one of those slow campers and he wouldn't use the turnout. Ah, but it's always worth it to come down and see you, Rachel. You got anything new in my line?"

The question precipitated a conversation of more than half an hour. Gil was an eclectic reader, and his line included disparate collecting interests ranging from western bird life to Civil War history. At the end of the conversation, with a stack of books Gil would be purchasing piled up on the desk at the front of the shop, he said tentatively, "Rachel, a friend of mine up in Idyllwild is trying to sell his library. I wonder if you'd like to come up and have a look at it some time."

Rachel smile. "Gil, are you talking about somebody with a garage full of *Reader's Digest Condensed Books*?"

"Come on, Rachel, we're not *all* Jud Cromptons up there. Would I ask you to drive two and a half hours just to look at something like that? This guy's got a sensational collection and a unique one, too, and all of a sudden, I don't know why, he's ready to sell it."

"Who is this person?"

"His name's Wilbur DeMarco."

"The mystery writer?"

Gil Franklin looked back at her blankly. "Gosh, not that I know of. As far as I know, old Wilbur's not any kind of a writer. Of course, you know, I don't read much in that field."

Rachel walked to the shelf of reference books behind her desk and pulled off a copy of Allen J. Hubin's crime fiction bibliography. She flipped through the pages until she found the listing for Wilbur DeMarco.

"Sure, here he is," she said. "He published all his books in the thirties. I had no idea he was still alive. I wonder why he quit writing." She pointed to the list as Gil looked over her shoulder. "See? His last book was published in 1937."

"Thirty-seven. Well, I'll be damned."

"Does that have some special significance?"

"Darned right it does. This collection I told you about covers all different fields, and nearly all of them are in mint condition, with dust jackets. The only thing they have in common is that every single book was published in 1937."

Rachel was intrigued. "I never heard of anybody collecting a single year before. It's an interesting approach, but I doubt if it's one that would appeal to many people."

"Well, you see, Rachel, Wilbur's got sort of a thing about 1937. In fact, if you went in his house, you'd see that all the furniture, all the appliances, all the magazines he's got lying around, everything in there dates from 1937 or earlier. He's got the shell of an old console radio. Hidden inside it is a cassette player, and he's got the biggest collection I ever saw of old radio shows—things like 'Fibber McGee and Molly,' Father Coughlin, Roosevelt's speeches, the Fitch Bandwagon, 'Amos 'n' Andy,' the 'Green Hornet,' 'The Shadow,' Jack Benny, 'Town Hall Tonight,' Lowell Thomas, the World Series, oh, you name it—every single one of them from 1937. He even drives around town in a '37 Duesenberg. Beautiful thing."

"Do you have any idea why he's so fixated on 1937?"

"No, I can't say that I do. You must think Wilbur is some kind of nut, and I guess in that one aspect of his life he *is* a little nutty. But otherwise he's just like anybody else up there. He'll turn out for the pancake breakfasts and spaghetti feeds and donate his share of money to the music school and get involved in civic activities. He's a very friendly and convivial sort of a guy. Except when he's inside his house, he's perfectly willing to live in 1987 with the rest of us. But then he goes behind those doors and—well, I've never been able to figure it out, Rachel. It's a puzzle to me."

"But now you say he wants to sell all of his 1937 books?"

"That's what he told me. In fact, it seems like all of a sudden he's decided to put 1937 behind him. Anyway, I think

10

you ought to get up there and have a look at his collection, Rachel, before some other dealer beats you to it, because, believe me, it's really something special."

"All right, Gil. You've been a good friend, and you wouldn't steer me wrong. I'll come up and have a look. When do you think would be a good time to come?"

"Well—" Gil looked a little sheepish. "I did tell Wilbur that I'd try to get you up there this Saturday. Of course, if Saturday isn't convenient for you . . ."

"No, no, Saturday sounds fine."

Gil looked out the window. "Good. Well, I guess it's time I got going. I want to beat the heavy traffic up to the hill."

Rachel's face furrowed slightly. She worried about the elderly man making that long drive to the mountains by himself. "Aren't you going to spend the night with your niece?"

"No, not today. I don't want to be too much of a burden, barging in on her all the time."

"But that's quite a difficult drive for . . ."

"For somebody my age? Is that what you were going to say?" Gil asked. "Look, I've been driving for over sixty years, and I'm a better driver than ninety percent of the people who share that road with me, so worry about them. Don't worry about me." He started to write a check for the purchases stacked in front of him. Then he stopped as another thought occurred to him. "Rachel, do you by any chance have any of Wilbur's books here in the store?"

"I think I have one." She walked back to her mystery fiction section and pulled down a copy of a book with an art-deco dust jacket typical of the 1930s. The title, Gil saw, was *Murder at the Snowline.*

"Well," said Gil, "I guess he was a mountain person even in those days, huh?" He looked at the book's jacket, then opened it to the back flap and looked at the photograph of the author. He snorted with laughter. "By gosh, that's how we all used to look back then, wasn't it? Get a load of that slicked-down hair. Yeah, you can tell that's old Wilbur, all right, if you look real close. Not sure if I'd know, though, if I didn't know—if you know what I mean. How much are you asking for this one, Rachel?"

She said, "The price should be in there." She looked at it and winced. "Fifteen dollars. You have to understand that a vintage mystery in this kind of condition . . ."

"Don't apologize," said Gil. "Don't apologize. I don't usually like detective stories, but this one's by somebody I know, I guess it's worth it to me. Heck, a *new* novel costs that much these days. I'll just add fifteen bucks and tax to my bill here." He quickly computed the addition in his head, wrote a check in an elegant script, and handed it across to Rachel. "Thanks a lot, Rachel. It's a pleasure, as always, and I'll tell Wilbur to expect you up there this Saturday, okay?"

"That's right. Now you be careful driving up that hill."

"Oh, I will. You don't have to worry about me."

When the lanky man had left, Rachel found herself feeling rather sheepish. It always embarrassed her to charge a collector's price to someone who was not collecting in that particular area and who just wanted to read the book. Also, she was a little sorry to see *Murder at the Snowline* go. Since she was going to meet Wilbur DeMarco on Saturday, she was interested in looking at one of his books herself. Well, maybe she could find one at the library.

That evening, Rachel sat at the table in the apartment she occupied above Vermilion's Bookshop. She was sharing a pizza with Stu Wellman of the Los Angeles *News-Canvass*. It was a Wednesday night tradition. Tonight she seemed to be nibbling at her food less enthusiastically than usual, and Stu could tell there was something on her mind.

"Okay, out with it, Rachel. What's bugging you?"

"Oh, nothing really, Stu. But a funny thing happened this afternoon. Gil Franklin was in. You remember, I introduced you to him once."

Stu nodded. "Sure. Terrific old guy."

"Gil knows a man up in Idyllwild named Wilbur DeMarco. He used to be a mystery writer back in the thirties, and he wants to sell his collection of books—every one of them published in 1937."

Stu shrugged. "So, he's got a nutty collecting interest. That's not so unusual. I mean you've told me about people who collect books with cars on the dust jacket, books with 'dog' in the title, books with titles from Shakespeare—" and Stu rattled off another half-dozen or so bizarre collecting interests that Rachel had mentioned to him over the course of their friendship. "So this guy collects books published in 1937. What's so strange about that? I mean, it's strange, but is it any stranger than any of those others?"

"He was a mystery writer. And his own last book was published in 1937. Stu, something terrible, or anyway major, must have happened to him in 1937. He quit writing, and in the years since, he's spent all his energy collecting 1937 memorabilia. Not just books, but all kinds of things. What do you suppose could have happened to him in 1937?"

"If he wanted to keep reliving it, it was probably some- thing *good*." Stu, in spite of himself, was beginning to get in- terested.

"Or something good *ended* for him then. Whatever it was, it soured him on mystery writing. Maybe it was a crime of some sort."

"You're jumping to conclusions. Lots of people have been mystery writers and gone on to something legitimate."

"I wonder what he's been doing all these years to support himself. Gil didn't tell me what he did for a living, just that he lives up in Idyllwild now. I'm going up there on Saturday to have a look at his books. Do you think you'd like to come, too?"

"Sure, why not? If the guy used to be a well-known writer, there might be a story in it for the paper."

"Of course, you understand, I don't want him to think I've brought you into it, to obligate him to give you an interview."

"If he doesn't want to be written about, then I won't write about him. I'll just come along for the ride, and if it looks like there's a story in it, I'll suggest something to him. If he doesn't want to go for it, then fine. Is that all right?"

"Sure, Stu, that's fine. I'd love to have you along." She paused a moment and then continued reflectively, "Exactly fifty years later he wants to get rid of those books. I wonder why, Stu. I wonder why he doesn't need them any more."

2

ON SATURDAY MORNING, Stu and Rachel set out for the small mountain town of Idyllwild. They started out in smog. The air was oppressive enough in Hollywood and didn't improve as they crossed into Riverside County, but leaving Banning and starting the winding drive up Highway 243, they left the bad air below them. It had been a warm day in the city. The springtime mountain air was cooler, and the drive was very pleasant. At tiny Lake Fulmor, they stopped to have their picnic lunch and watch people fishing along both banks. Rachel had never had the desire to fish herself but found it restful seeing others do it—just as long as they were unsuccessful. Fish out of water she found depressing.

Finally, at a little bit above the 5,000-foot level, they arrived in the center of Idyllwild. Gil Franklin had assured them it would be impossible to find Wilbur DeMarco's house without a guide, so he had arranged to meet them at one o'clock in front of one of the town's numerous real-estate offices. As Rachel didn't discover until she and Stu got out of the car to stretch their legs, Acorn Realty was the headquarters of Jud Crompton.

"Well, hello, Rachel!" Crompton walked from the doorway of the realty office over to the car, the picture of cordiality. But his outward good humor had an edge to it. "How are you today?"

"Just fine. Uh, Stu Wellman, this is Jud Crompton."

"Glad to know you, Stu. Didn't know you knew my name, Rachel. I didn't introduce myself before I walked out of your shop the other day, did I? Maybe you and Gil had a few choice words to say about me?" He raised his hands, still with a broad smile on his face. "Oh, I know I deserved it. I'm sorry about that, but I can get a little irate at times. Especially when I know I'm right."

Rachel suppressed a laugh at the backhanded apology.

"Are you a bibliophile, Stu?" Crompton asked.

"Depends on what you mean by bibliophile. I read a lot of books, but I'm more interested in the text than anything else."

"Well, I collect first editions." Crompton's manner was incredibly self-important. "That copy of *Time and Again* I brought you the other day, Rachel, I sold for thirty-five bucks to a dealer not ten blocks from you. Good deal for him really. He's probably sold it by now for sixty or seventy-five." Rachel wondered if this was the truth or a face-saving invention. She didn't doubt it could be true. There were naive newcomers in every business, and not long ago she'd been one herself.

Crompton said, "What's your line of work, Stu?"

"I'm a reporter. On the L.A. *News-Canvass.*"

"Good paper. Better than the *Times* in general makeup and layout I always thought. Scooped 'em a few times, too. You up here on a story, or ... ?"

"Just a day's outing."

"Well, if you have any questions about the local flora and fauna, just stop by the office here."

Crompton's attention was diverted by a young couple studying the homes-for-sale pictured in his window. With another tight, vaguely insincere smile, he said, "Got to get back to work. They look like a couple of live ones. After a while, you can tell." Rachel reflected that the househunters would probably be all right, as long as he didn't try to sell them any first editions.

As Crompton left them, Rachel and Stu saw Gil Franklin walking toward the car briskly. "Hi, folks! Sorry if I'm a little late, but I decided I'd walk in from my place. Lots of traffic

16

in town weekends."

Stu looked up and down the quiet street and said, "Right. Looks like the Santa Ana Freeway at rush hour."

Gil jumped into Stu's car and gave them directions to De-Marco's place. Within a block, even the Idyllwild version of urban bustle disappeared, and the squirrels were the only competing traffic. By the third turn, Stu was convinced he had needed a guide, not only to find DeMarco's house, but also to find Idyllwild again.

Between giving directions, Gil provided Rachel with a running account of the local bird life, pointing out a nuthatch, a Steller's jay, a scrubjay, a black-hooded junco, and an acorn woodpecker engaged in his favorite activity. Concentrating on the winding road, Stu missed the birds but knew he'd never remember their names anyway. The Wellman family had never produced many outdoorsmen or bird-watchers.

DeMarco's house was on the edge of the hill, with a fine view of the National Forest on one side and the local land-mark, Tacquitz Rock, on the other. The neighboring houses were comfortably far away and virtually hidden in the trees.

Wilbur DeMarco, who appeared to greet them as soon as Stu pulled into the driveway, was about the same age as Gil Franklin, around eighty. He was a smaller man, stocky, energetic and cordial. He ushered them into his home. The ground floor of the two-story house was basically one room, with the kitchen area to the right and a fireplace to the left. Large windows on the back and side walls made the most of the view, and doors on each side led to a wooden deck that ran around three sides of the house.

Though Stu and Rachel had been somewhat prepared for what they would find, they still were astonished at how completely Wilbur DeMarco had managed to evoke the thir-ties in the furnishings and decorations. There was a hand-some photograph of President Franklin D. Roosevelt over the fireplace. An old console radio dominated the room, and

17

if it was really a cassette player, that fact and the cassettes to feed it were kept well out of sight. Several issues of *Time* and *Life*, all with 1937 dates, lay on the coffee table. The long, comfortable-looking couch and matching armchairs also evoked the period in a way hard to pin down. A record cabinet held several albums of old-fashioned seventy-eights.

A huge, glassed-in bookcase in the far left corner of the room, backing on the stairway, held the treasures Rachel was most interested in. She could recognize the books with a glance as nineteen-thirties in origin, but she had rarely seen so many that old in such fine, even mint condition, almost all of them with their original dust jackets. There was Kenneth Roberts's *Northwest Passage*, A.J. Cronin's *The Citadel*, W. Somerset Maugham's *Theatre*, John Steinbeck's *Of Mice and Men*, James M. Cain's *Serenade*, and C.S. Forester's Horatio Hornblower novel, *Beat to Quarters*. Such a nice copy as that one could bring a good price.

DeMarco's mystery-writing colleagues were represented, too, though not in the numbers Rachel might have expected—next to the writer's own 1937 novel, *Murder Threw Friday*, were Ellery Queen's *The Door Between*, Dorothy L. Sayers's *Busman's Honeymoon*, Agatha Christie's *Cards on the Table*, and Anthony Boucher's *The Case of the Seven of Calvary*. On another shelf was nonfiction—that venerable chestnut, *How to Win Friends and Influence People* by Dale Carnegie; Noel Coward's autobiographical *Present Indicative*; Clarence Day's *Life with Mother*; *You Have Seen Their Faces*, the photo essay on Southern sharecroppers by Erskine Caldwell and Margaret Bourke-White; Walter Lippmann's *Inquiry Into the Principles of the Good Society*. Rachel didn't doubt for a moment that all these books were 1937 first editions, and they could scarcely have looked newer and crisper in a 1937 bookshop.

She tried to view them with a professional eye. If the phrase "Pretty Pearl" appeared on page nineteen of DeMarco's copy of John P. Marquand's *The Late George Apply*, it was the true first and worth about a hundred dollars. The Steinbeck book was worth two to three hundred. But her mental cash register was overwhelmed by the sheer wonder of the collection.

Stu, meanwhile, had found what appeared to be a mid-1937 edition of the Los Angeles daily *Times*. But the pages didn't look yellowed the way those of an old newspaper would. The paper could have been thrown in Wilbur De-Marco's driveway that morning. He must have had reprints made for him specially—how much expense had the man gone to in indulging his hobby? If it was only a hobby.

Stu asked the obvious question after polite greetings and expressions of wonder had been exchanged. "Why such an interest in 1937, Mr. DeMarco?"

The man's smile seemed almost triumphant. But if it was, he didn't explain. "It was just an interesting year," he said. "A lot of memorable things happened in 1937. Jack Benny and Fred Allen had their feud; President Roosevelt was trying to pack the Supreme Court and Congress wouldn't let him; there was a coronation in Britain of King George VI, and, of course, you know all about what happened to his predecessor; there were all kinds of strikes going on; War Admiral won the Triple Crown; Jean Harlow died; the President of I.B.M. was decorated by Adolph Hitler; Hugo Black got named to the Supreme Court, and people found out he'd been a member of the Ku Klux Klan; Amelia Earhart vanished; the Golden Gate bridge opened; Orson Welles put on a modern-dress *Julius Caesar* set in fascist Italy. It was just a real significant and colorful year, that's all, and I didn't know anybody else that was collecting a year, so I thought it would be fun."

Stu said, " 'Thirty-seven was the same year you stopped writing mystery novels, too, wasn't it?"

DeMarco seemed untroubled by Stu's probing. "Well, I just decided to go on to doing something else, that's all. Nothing sinister about it." He smiled slightly. "You're not a reporter by any chance, are you?"

Stu said, "Okay, yeah, I work for the Los Angeles *News-Canvass*. They probably don't throw it up here."

"They don't throw anything up here," Gil said quickly. "Except the bull, that is. If you want a paper, you have to pick one up in town. Of course, you have to go into town for your mail anyway. They don't make mail deliveries up here, either. Everybody has a box at the post office."

Wilbur DeMarco obviously saw Gil's dissertation as an attempt to avoid the subject of Stu's profession. He said, "But whatever they throw or don't throw, you *are* a reporter."

"I am, but I just came along with Rachel. If you don't want any publicity—"

DeMarco shook his head. "No, I don't want any publicity! But if I did want any publicity, you'd be glad to give me some, right?"

"Well, sure. I think this collection of yours is fascinating. I never saw anything quite like it."

DeMarco shook his head again. "No publicity! And that is final. Now, Miss Hennings, would you like to start having a look at the books? If you care to make me an offer for the whole lot, they're yours. You can carry them away, today. I'm done with them. Just say which ones you want."

"Don't you have any interest in keeping them unified as a collection, Mr. DeMarco?"

"No, not necessarily. If I did, I'd be in touch with the universities, but it'd take too damned long. If you only want certain ones, you just pick 'em out and take those. But I would rather you'd take the lot, and I'm ready to bargain."

"You're just not interested in them any more?"

"No, my interest in 1937 has waned a bit. By morning, it may be gone completely. As a matter of fact, I'm going to have a garage sale here tomorrow."

"A garage sale, huh?" said Gil. "Now you're talking! Garage sales are big up here in Idyllwild, Rachel, you'd be surprised. You're not going to include the books in the garage

20

sale, are you?"

"I just might if Miss Hennings doesn't want 'em. I want to move this stuff out of here fast. Everything goes."

"What are you going to do with the house, Wilbur?" Gil asked. "Are you going to sell all your furniture?"

"Oh, I'll probably keep a bed, and a few other essentials. But all the 1937 stuff goes."

"How about the Duesenburg?"

"Already sold. Fellow from Newport Beach drove it off the hill a couple weeks ago. Sorry to disappoint you if you wanted it, Gil."

"Nope, I'll sort of miss seeing you tooling around town in it, but I've got no desire to drive around in anything that much more valuable than me. Terrible responsibility. If I drove it up here, I'd worry about scraping it, and if I drove it down to L.A. I'd worry about somebody stealing it from me."

"Can't say I blame you," DeMarco said with a grin. "I felt that way myself. I had a notice about the sale run in the *Town Crier* last Thursday, so I'm expecting a good turnout. But you tell all your friends, Gil, make sure nobody misses it. I don't want to have anything left here by Sunday night. Gonna sell things at bargain-basement prices."

Rachel said, "You know, if you'd wait a little bit longer, and notify some of the real collectors and dealers in these various areas, you could get some big prices. Why, even that old refrigerator. I'll bet there are collectors who would pay a lot of money for that. I don't think I'd just let it all go in a garage sale."

DeMarco shook his head. "Naw, I don't want to go to the trouble. Look, Miss Hennings, I don't need a lot of money. I've got everything I need, and I've got no heirs to think about, just my cousin Arthur, who's better off than I am. I'm a contented man. I just want to unload all this 1937 stuff 'cause I don't need it any more."

"Why don't you need it any more?" Stu asked.

Rachel said, "Now, Stu, don't pry into Mr. DeMarco's private affairs. He doesn't have to tell us if he doesn't want to."

"There's nothing to tell," insisted DeMarco. "I just decided once upon a time to collect 1937; I collected it to the utmost. Now I'm going to go on and collect something else, maybe beer cans, maybe Tiffany lamps. Maybe I'll collect 1938," he added, with a wink.

"Or maybe you'll go back to mystery writing," Stu suggested.

DeMarco shook his head. "That's not likely."

As Rachel began her intensive study of the book collection, DeMarco offered them something to drink. Rachel and Gil opted for iced tea, while Stu agreed to join his host in a beer. He was rather disappointed to find it was not a 1937 vintage out of a collectible bottle but a boring 1980s light.

As the afternoon went on, Stu spent some time helping to peruse the books, the rest of the time looking around the front room and exchanging desultory conversation with Gil and DeMarco. One exhibit over the fireplace particularly intrigued him: an old Planter's Peanuts can, a model of a '30s vintage Chevrolet, a pair of ticket stubs from the Criterion Theater in New York, and a key with the name of the Hotel Astor on the tag.

"Uh, Mr. DeMarco, what's the connection here?"

"Connection?"

"Between the peanuts and the car and the hotel key and the tickets."

"Why should there be any connection? Except that they're all *bona fide* 1937 relics, like everything else here."

"The way they're sort of joined together, separate from everything else, I just thought there must be a connection of some sort."

Wilbur DeMarco's smile had something secretive in it, Stu thought. But he continued blandly refusing to offer any enlightenment. DeMarco was a cordial host, but it was obvious he would stonewall any questions about his odd hobby beyond the superficial.

Rachel, quickly looking through the books and appraising their value, was oblivious to the conversation. As promised, they were in all fields and included many of the most significant titles published in 1937, along with more esoteric tomes and some representative junk. She weighed in her mind what kind of an offer DeMarco might accept and also how high she could afford to go. Apparently she had to make the offer today or the deal would be off. She wondered when a mint first edition of Steinbeck's *Of Mice and Men* had last been offered in a garage sale.

Finally, she came up with a four-digit figure for the whole collection that she thought was relatively fair to DeMarco and that would allow her to make a reasonable profit when she got in touch with collectors and dealers in the individual subject areas. DeMarco accepted the offer immediately. Between them, Rachel and Stu managed to pack the collection into several boxes DeMarco had ready and squeeze them into the trunk and back seat of Stu's car. Rachel wrote a check, and the deal was concluded.

Just as they were leaving, Stu said, "You're sure you aren't going to go back to writing detective stories, Mr. DeMarco?"

"Not after fifty years. They don't write my kind any more."

"These days they write all kinds," Rachel said.

DeMarco had the same secretive smile he'd worn when Stu had asked him about his mantelpiece exhibit. "You think authorship of detective stories is a permanent condition, do you, one of those things that gets in your blood?"

"Sure," Stu said. "Why not? Like bookselling and journalism."

"Well, you may just be right about that. I sometimes find myself thinking in puzzles. If I write any more detective stories, though, it won't be for public consumption."

After they'd said goodbye and were driving Gil back to his own house on the hill, Rachel said, "What do you suppose he meant by that? Not for public consumption, I mean."

Stu said, "Write them for his own amusement and stick

them in a drawer, I guess. Sort of a mystery-writing Emily Dickinson."

"I doubt that somehow." After a moment's pensive silence, she asked, "Stu, do you have to go back to L.A. today?"

"No," he said, "I don't suppose I have to."

"Why don't we stay over and go to the garage sale tomorrow?"

Stu shrugged. "Sure, if you want. If you buy anything, though, you're not going to be able to cram it into my car. The books are taking all the space there is."

Gil pointed out, "You could fill up the space where I'm sitting."

Rachel laughed. "I don't want to buy anything else. But I think I'd like to have a look at what he has for sale, and maybe a look at some of the people who come to buy. There's quite a senior-citizen population up here, isn't there, Gil?"

"Sure, all sorts of people come up here to retire. There's not a lot of business up here, and it's real hard to work on the hill and live on the hill, too. Most younger residents have to commute down to Banning or Hemet. But for somebody who's retired, it's ideal. The best thing about it, there's *no* skiing and it's not on the way to anywhere, so it hasn't got overdeveloped yet. It's still the kind of a friendly, rural place that it's always been. It should stay that way for quite a few years. We have to fight the developers like anybody else . . . Anyway, yeah, there are a lot of senior citizens. What's your point?"

"People who might remember 1937 would be interested in DeMarco's memorabilia. And I'd like to talk to some of them. Stu, wouldn't it be a good story for the paper, too?"

"Wait a second," said Stu. "I promised I wouldn't sic any publicity on DeMarco without his permission, so it's all off the record as far as I'm concerned."

"Idyllwild might make a good subject for an article. Get some of these people's memories on tape. I wish I'd done that with my own parents and grandparents, but I never had the chance."

"With my family, I always wanted to turn *off* the flood of memories. It got to be a real bore."

"You're just a cynic, Stu. If you'd asked them the right questions, they'd have been fascinating."

Stu shook his head. "Not my family."

"Gil, where's a good place for us to spend the night?"

"You can get a cabin over at the Idyllwild Inn if you want to. Or for that matter, you can stay with me. I've got plenty of room."

"That would be wonderful, if it's not too much trouble for you."

"No trouble at all. It'd be fun to have you around." Gil looked at them appraisingly. "Now I know you young folks don't look at things exactly the same way as my generation. If I offered you separate rooms, you might be insulted. On the other hand, if I offered you the same room, you might be scandalized. I don't know the exact nature of your friendship, you understand. But whatever arrangements you want to make are okay with me. If the missus were still alive, we'd have to proceed with a little more caution." Gil was looking embarrassed, which Rachel thought was a bit disingenuous of him.

"Gil," she said, "one room will be all that we'll require."

"That's just what I figured."

3

THE FOLLOWING MORNING, the three of them were in front of Wilbur DeMarco's house at 10 A.M., the scheduled time for the beginning of his 1937 garage sale. But the garage door was still closed and there was no sign of a sale taking place. Several other people, most of them of the same generation as Gil and Wilbur, were milling around in front of the house.

Gil greeted one of them, an elderly woman with snow-white hair. "Hi, there, Dorie," Gil said. "I'd like to introduce you to a couple of flatlander friends of mine, Rachel Hennings and Stu Wellman. Folks, this is Dorie Moss. You came for Wilbur's sale, huh?"

"Sure did," said Dorie Moss, "and I have to say I'm a little worried. It's not like him not to start on time."

"He probably just overslept," said Gil. "So what'd you come lookin' for, Dorie? Got your eye on anything special?"

She looked around furtively. "Well, I don't know that I want to say. Might be somebody else after it, too. Actually, it may sound funny, but it's that old toaster of his. I used to have a toaster like that, and it made the best toast I ever had in my life, not like any of these newfangled ones do. He told me it still worked. I'd like to look at the other things, too. You know, it brings back memories of the old days. You can understand that."

While Dorie was speaking, an elderly black man as tall and thin as Gil had joined the group. "I just want to know if his records are in the sale," he told them. "That man has some jazz collection. Priceless stuff, old seventy-eights. Can't imagine he'd want to give it up, but if he does, here I am."

"I think everything goes, Ernest," Gil said. He introduced the man as Ernest Basset. "Used to be a dancer," Gil added.

"Used to be? What's this used-to-be stuff? How'd you like it if I said you used to be a Civil War scholar?"

"Okay, okay. Ernest is still a dancer. He used to be a *good* dancer."

The black man laughed. "Oh, yeah, I used to be almost as good as Jud Crompton." At that, they both laughed, but offered no explanation of what must have been a local joke. "How long you folks going to be up here?"

"Just for the weekend," Rachel said.

"Too bad. You come to our annual Town Prom next Saturday, and I'd show you just how good a dancer I still am."

"Town Prom?"

"It's a good cause, benefits ISOMATA."

"A disease?" Stu ventured.

"Idyllwild School of Music and the Arts. Most cultural thing we got up here and we like to keep it healthy."

"What's keeping Wilbur, anyhow?" Gil said. He walked up to the door and pushed the doorbell. When there was no response, he tried it several times more, with no better result.

"I really am worried, Gil," said Dorie. "He could be sick or something."

Ernest Basset said, "Heck, Wilbur's as healthy as anybody I know."

"Yes, I know, Ernest, but people our age, you never know when something might happen."

The other half-dozen people gathered to wait for the sale had now joined the group near the door. There was one less-than-senior citizen among them, a dramatically handsome and muscular man of about thirty in shorts and a sweatshirt. Since they'd arrived, he had been eying Rachel and Stu had been eying him. "I think we should break the door in," he said now.

"Break it in?" said another man, a tanned and athletic

27

seventy year old. "Roger, you don't just break into a man's house."

"You do to save his life, Jack!" Dorie Moss snapped.

Gil was starting to look a little worried himself. "Well, what do you think, folks? Shall we try it?"

Stu Wellman nodded. "I think we probably should, if we can. He might need our help." He noticed an unscreened side window that was slightly open. "You folks up here aren't too security-conscious, are you?" he said, easily pushing the window up from outside.

"Most people on the hill don't even lock their front doors," said Gil. "This is an old-time small-town environment."

Stu climbed through the window and opened the front door from the inside to let Gil, Rachel, and Dorie in. "Why don't the rest of you folks stay out here," Stu said. "We'll call you if we need you." No one objected to the idea.

The four of them looked around at the living room. Gil called out tentatively, "Wilbur? You home, Wilbur?" There was no sign that any preparation had been made for the day's garage sale. The only things obviously missing from the room were the books that Stu and Rachel had packed up and removed the day before. But then Stu noticed that the odd little arrangement on the mantel was gone as well.

Stu started up the stairs, calling, "Mr. DeMarco? Mr. De-Marco, are you here?" At the top of the stairs he found the master bedroom. It too was decorated and furnished in purely thirties style. The bed was neatly made, the room was empty. Stu finished a quick survey of the top floor, and was just starting down the stairs again, when he heard a quavering scream from below. He rushed down the stairs and across to the kitchen where the other three were standing. Rachel had her arms around Dorie Moss.

"He's here," Rachel said in a shaky voice, and nodded to the spot where, between a stove, a refrigerator and a sink, all of which had been state-of-the-art in the year 1937, was

28

the body of Wilbur DeMarco in a pool of blood. It appeared the former mystery writer had been shot to death in his 1937 house.

After using DeMarco's telephone to call the Riverside County Sheriff's Department, Stu and the others waited outside with the others who had gathered for the sale, leaving whatever evidence could be found in the house undisturbed. Stu suggested that everyone stay in the event police wanted to question them. He had no way of holding them, of course, but, whether out of good citizenship or curiosity, no one seemed inclined to leave.

A few minutes after the discovery of DeMarco's body, Jud Crompton pulled up in a big late-model Buick. "Where's the sale, folks?" he boomed.

Dorie Moss, who seemed more grieved at DeMarco's death than anyone else, snapped at him, "The sale is off, Jud. Somebody's killed Wilbur."

"Killed him? I don't believe it."

"Well, you'd better."

"I was hoping I could buy some of his books."

"They were already sold, Jud," said Gil Franklin, with a kind of malicious pleasure.

"Already sold?" He looked at Rachel, light dawning behind his cold eyes. "Oh, I get it. That's what you're doing up here. But that's no fair, jumping the sale."

The athletic older man called Jack snarled, "A man's dead, Crompton! Doesn't that mean anything to you?"

"Well, of course it does. I'm offended you'd think it doesn't. I liked Wilbur DeMarco as much as anybody. He was a friend of mine." Rachel hoped the realtor wasn't about to manufacture a tear for the occasion. "Sheriff's been notified?"

"All taken care of," Gil assured him.

"Good. Well, I have to go. This is sure a sad occasion."

"Sure," Gil said inaudibly to the realtor's retreating back.

"Nothing to keep you here."

Ernest Basset said, "He's probably thinkin' about how he can get the listing right now."

Fifteen minutes later, a deputy named Adam Kane arrived. He was a tall, good-looking, fortyish man, and every move he made impressed Stu and Rachel with his efficiency. "Lucky I was on the hill," he said, "or I wouldn't have been here this quick."

After a brief inspection of the murder scene, Kane dispatched two other deputies to search the area around De-Marco's house for the weapon, which was probably a handgun. Soon various Riverside County Sheriff's Department technicians started arriving from Hemet to take part in the investigation.

The people who had been waiting for the sale were questioned one by one and released, with the four who had actually entered the house detained until last. It wasn't long before the deputy figured he had the answer. "Kids," he said. "Kids looking for drugs. They thought the house was empty when they broke in, the old guy confronted 'em, they shot him. The kind of tragedy I see every day. More often down the hill than up here, I have to admit, but it's been known to happen."

"Not enough police protection, that's why," Gil Franklin said irritably.

"So you think it's as simple as that?" Rachel said.

"I don't know if you'd call it simple or not, Miss, but I'm pretty sure that's what happened. Whether we'll get the kid or not, who knows? I tell you, these junkies."

Even when Stu told him about the odd group of items missing from the mantelpiece, Adam Kane didn't seem to want to look beyond the burglary theory to any more personal motive for Wilbur DeMarco's death. Rachel, though, was not satisfied with the deputy's easy explanation, and she told Stu and Gil why as they were driving back to Gil's house after a couple of hours' questioning by the police.

30

"Don't you see how all this fits together?" she said.

"I don't see how anything fits together at all," Gil replied.

"Well, look, he spent all these years collecting 1937 memorabilia, arranging for himself virtually to live in the year 1937. And then suddenly he lost interest in it. Now why would he do that?"

Both older and younger men returned blank stares. "I guess you better tell us, Rachel," Stu said.

"I'll tell you. Something happened in 1937, some terrible experience, possibly a crime. I think it ruined Wilbur De-Marco's life, or radically changed it, anyway. Certainly it soured him on writing detective stories, and I think he spent all of that time since trying to work out that particular terrible event. Maybe it was a murder, maybe it was the murder of his wife or someone he cared for, and maybe he spent all these years trying to solve it, and maybe the way he saw to solve it was to steep himself in everything that he associated with that year."

"Rachel," said Stu, "that's a pretty farfetched theory."

"Of course, it's a farfetched theory," she said, "but it's a farfetched bunch of circumstances. Don't you think it's quite a coincidence that a man spends all his life collecting 1937 memorabilia, then suddenly loses interest in it, and as soon as he loses interest in it, he dies, murdered? And it wasn't by some kid junkie, I can tell you that!"

"Well, what's your explanation?" Gil asked.

"To me it's perfectly obvious. He solved his mystery. He found out what really happened in 1937, and once he did that, he didn't need his 1937 memorabilia any more. But of course, once he solved it he became a danger to somebody else. One of these other senior citizens living here in Idyllwild. He had discovered their culpability in that crime of 1937. And so naturally he put himself in danger. The murderer had to eliminate him before he could reveal anything about the earlier crime."

Gil looked at her with a satirical expression on his face.

"Rachel, just how many of those detective stories in your stock do you read?"

"I read a few. Not more than a couple a week, though."

"Well, what you're telling me sounds just like the plot of one of those detective stories, from around about Wilbur's vintage as a matter of fact."

"But all the *circumstances* sound just like the plot of one of those detective stories, too. And what was all that stuff about writing detective stories but not for public consumption? And what was the point of his little sly smiles when Stu asked him about that stuff on the mantelpiece? He was cooking something up, and he expected to bring it all to a climax last night, before his garage sale. Remember? He said his interest in 1937 was waning and by morning it should be gone completely. I'm just responding to what's here, Gil!"

Stu was a bit closer to being convinced by Rachel's arguments. "You know, we shouldn't dismiss this out of hand, Gil. Rachel does have a little experience in these lines. She also has some special talents that you may not know about."

Stu and Rachel exchanged a secretive glance. Gil had no idea what the glance indicated. Maybe Rachel fancied herself some kind of amateur detective. It was more than that, but Stu and Rachel were not about to reveal it.

"You know," said Gil, "whether you're right or not, I seriously doubt that Adam Kane is going to take that tack in solving the case. He's convinced he's got a junkie killer."

"Were there signs of anyone having broken in?" Rachel asked.

"I don't think he found any, no. But the thing of it is, as I told you before, a lot of us are careless about locking our doors up here. Heck, the junkie could have just walked in when he thought nobody was home and got surprised by Wilbur. No offense, but I think Adam's theory makes lots more sense than yours does."

"Too much coincidence," said Rachel.

"Life is full of coincidence."

"Yes, I know it is." Another idea occurred to her. "If I were one of Wilbur's local acquaintances, not a young junkie, and I'd killed him last night, I wonder if I'd turn out this morning as if I were expecting his sale to go ahead."

"The murderer returns to the scene of the crime, huh?" Stu said skeptically.

"That's just an old saw, but in this case, it might make sense. Diverts suspicion, don't you think?"

"Rachel, I wish you'd leave this stuff to the pros."

"Stu, you pointed out yourself those items that were missing from the mantelpiece. Doesn't that mean there's more behind this than just a junkie?"

"Not necessarily. Wilbur might have moved them himself, getting ready for the sale."

"Nothing else seemed to have been disturbed. Gil, tell us something more about the people that were waiting outside Wilbur's house. Did you know them all?"

"Most of them. Ernest and Dorie I introduced to you. Jack Hooper is a nice fellow, physical fitness buff. He was some kind of top athlete years ago, competed in the Olympics in fact. 'Thirty-six, I guess."

"Any connection to Wilbur?"

"Not that I know of, except that they knew each other. The young fellow is Roger Payne. He lives with his mother, Frances Payne."

"The movie actress?" Stu asked.

"You're quite a buff if you remember her. I think young Roger was taking quite a shine to you, Rachel."

Stu said, "Only natural he'd fix his eyes on the only young woman present."

"Thanks a lot for that tribute to my beauty," Rachel said. "You said Ernest Basset was a dancer. Was he on the stage?"

"Vaudeville mostly. But I think he did some picture work in the '30s."

"Another movie connection . . . I wonder if Wilbur De-Marco ever worked in movies."

"Beats me," Gil said. "Don't forget, I didn't even know he was a writer until you told me so."

"Did you read his book yet?"

"Part of it. I guess he wrote well enough, but that's not really my kind of story."

"Somebody should investigate all these people for their connections to Wilbur," Rachel said.

"You think it's likely they will with a ready-made run-of-the-mill burglary solution?" Stu said.

"No. You're probably right to think that deputy won't be quite that imaginative. And he may be right, of course. He has a lot of experience to go by."

If anyone thought Rachel had talked herself out of her theory, she soon exploded the notion. "I wish I could find out what really happened myself." Suddenly her eyes lit up. "You know what I could do if I had a little time?"

"What's that?" Stu asked.

"That article I was talking about yesterday. Recorded memories of all the senior citizens in Idyllwild. What a great cover for an investigation. Besides that it would be fun, too!"

Stu looked apprehensive, "Well, it's too bad you don't have time to do that. You do have to run the bookstore, don't you?"

"You know I haven't been doing too badly with that shop. I've even managed to hire on an employee."

"Yeah, that library school student."

Gil thought he detected a glint of jealousy in the reporter's eyes.

"I don't think he'd mind a few extra hours after his current quarter is finished," Rachel said. "He's gotten so good at it, he could probably run the store himself for a couple of weeks, and I could afford to spend my time up here and work on my article." She looked at their worried, doubtful faces and added placatingly, "You know, Stu, you and Gil are probably right. There's probably nothing to my idea. It's probably ridiculous. But even if it is, and even if nothing comes of it as far as solving the crime is concerned, wouldn't some reminiscences by the people up here be interesting?"

"Yeah, they would. But don't you think they're going to be a tad suspicious if you ask them all that they were doing in 1937?"

"Not at all. I wouldn't have to conceal anything. I could connect it up with Wilbur DeMarco's collecting interest. I know what I could do! I could tell them I was going to put together a collection of remembrances of 1937, and it was going to be a memorial to Wilbur DeMarco."

"You think people would swallow that?" Stu said.

"Why shouldn't they swallow it? Of course, if the person who murdered him is one of the people I interview, *that* person might not swallow it. But he or she would have to go along with it or else they'd look too suspicious. So I'd be able to get their remembrances, too. I could ask them all what they were doing in 1937. Find out how well they knew Wilbur DeMarco and what connection they'd had with him. Of course, I'd do a lot of research in the library first, about Wilbur's life—I'm sure he must be in some biographical sources—and then I'd know exactly what did happen to him in 1937 and how to slant my questions to people when I'm doing the interviews. Stu, you'd help me out, wouldn't you?"

Not answering the direct pleas, Stu tried another evasive action. "Look, Rachel, if you ask people what they were doing in a particular year, how would they remember?"

"What do you mean?"

"Well, let's test it. If I asked you what you were doing in 1977, could you tell me?"

"Well, not right off the bat. But if I had time to think about it beforehand, I could probably come up with something. And it would depend on what happened to me or to the world in that year. Most people who were alive then could probably zero in on 1963 pretty easily because they would tie their own memories to the Kennedy assassination. The same with 1941, because of Pearl Harbor. Now, 1937 didn't have any events quite *that* cataclysmic, but there were some memorable things."

"Nothing special happened to you in 1977, though?"

"Let's see, I was in high school . . ."

"And anyway, that's a recent year. What about a year half a century ago if you're a person of seventy or eighty?"

"The old days are easier to remember," Gil said. "Everybody knows that."

"All right then. What were *you* doing in 1937, Gil?"

"Well, let's see. In '37, I'd'a been 31 years old. I was teaching high-school history in a little town in Oklahoma, on the Ohio River. It wasn't a good year to be in that part of the country. In February, the river overflowed and inundated the school, along with nearly everybody's house, and when we about had that under control, there were the dust storms. We got through it somehow, but I never want to see that kind of thing again. As a schoolteacher, I was watching all the controversy over the Supreme Court very closely, along with other current events. I remarked on these things in class from time to time, and I remember the principal called me in to give me a lecture. I don't remember the gist of it too well, except that things had to have happened a certain amount of time ago to be history, and Mr. Roosevelt and his Supreme Court weren't quite ago enough. I asked him what *was* ago enough and he told me the World War—we'd only had one then—was probably safe, but don't have too much to say about the League of Nations. At that point, I had too much to say to the principal, and I was out of a job come June. So then I moved out here and I'm glad I did. I can produce more details on request if that's not a convincing enough sample."

"That settles that then," Rachel said, abandoning her attempt to dredge up memories of 1977, which she was sure had been a fairly boring adolescent year anyway. "I could go through all the old newspapers for 1937—steep myself in the period just the way Wilbur DeMarco did. As a matter of fact,

36

I could even live in his 1937 house!"

"Now wait a minute, Rachel," Stu said, "don't let's get carried away here. You want to live all alone in the house where this guy got murdered?"

"I'd rather have you come up and live with me there, Stu."

"But I can't come and live with you in the house, much as I'd love to. I have to work for a living. You seem to be doing so great with that bookshop that you can go off and leave for two weeks any time the whim strikes you, but the *News-Canvass* won't let me do that."

"Do you happen to know, Gil, who Wilbur DeMarco's heir would be?"

"No idea, Rachel. He didn't have any relatives that I know of."

"He mentioned a cousin," Stu provided, somewhat reluctantly. "Name's Arthur something."

"I wonder if I could arrange to rent the house for a couple of weeks, once the sheriff's department is through with it, of course. If there was an heir who wanted to come in and move everything out, maybe I could make some kind of arrangement. Did either of you ever read Jack Finney's *Time and Again*?"

"That book Crompton tried to sell you?" Gil said. "No, I haven't."

"It's all about time-travel. A man steeps himself in the atmosphere of the 1880s—the magazines and newspapers, the furniture, the decorations—and one day, he opens his door and he finds he's *living* in New York of the 1880s."

"I get it," Stu said. "So if you vanish in Wilbur DeMarco's house, we can look for you in 1937, huh?"

"I almost wish I could believe that. But only almost. Stu, maybe we should move all those 1937 books back into the house."

Stu groaned. "This is the most cockeyed idea I've ever heard of, and I won't be a party to it."

"Oh, then you won't help me? Well, okay, I'll just have to

manage it on my own, then."

"No, no, look I'll help you with research, but . . ."

"Once I've found all I can about Wilbur DeMarco, Stu, I'll bet you all the research I need is right there in that house. Somewhere in that house is whatever it was that allowed him to solve his mystery. If he can find it, then I can find it, too. I could invite those people there one by one and interview them right there in Wilbur's living room, surrounded by all that 1937 memorabilia. Why, they'd be so thrilled to see somebody of my generation interested in their past lives, and they'd be so interested in all that stuff that he put together— they'd really enjoy it, Stu. Maybe the murderer would even enjoy it!"

"That's just terrific, you and the murderer having a great time hashing over the good old days. Well, I'm not going to enjoy it. I'm going to be sitting down there in my office at the *News-Canvass* worrying about you. Don't you realize that if you actually did get on to something, the person who was the object of it might want to kill you, too?"

"No, he wouldn't dare. Besides, I'd make sure somebody knew who I was scheduled to interview at any given time. Nobody would be able to get away with it."

"If they *do* it," Stu pointed out, "what would it matter to you whether they get away with it or not?"

Rachel ignored the question. "Besides, I wouldn't have to let on that I'd figured out anything, and who would think that I'd be likely to anyway? All I'm doing is asking them to go back fifty years into the past." She smiled at Gil. "I'd have to check regularly with somebody who did live then so I could know whether my conclusions were correct or not. You'll cooperate with me won't you, Gil?"

"Rachel, I'll be glad to cooperate with you, but I'd much rather you stayed here with me than try to rent Wilbur's place. It sounds to me like one of those things where some- body wants to spend the night in the haunted house."

"Oh, is it haunted, too?" Rachel asked sweetly.

"Well, if it wasn't haunted before, it might just be haunted now," Gil said.

4

ON MONDAY, RACHEL was back in Vermilion's Bookshop on
Santa Monica Boulevard. She had called the UCLA library
school student who was her regular relief clerk and arranged
with him to work full-time for a couple of weeks beginning
the following Monday, while she took what she described as
a little vacation up to the mountains. Then she began scour-
ing the reference books for all the information she could find
about Wilbur DeMarco. And despite his reservations, Stu
was doing the same thing at the newspaper morgue at the
Los Angeles *News-Canvass*, where he was book editor and
general assignment reporter. Soon they had put together a
somewhat sketchy account of Wilbur DeMarco's life up
through 1937.

Wilbur had been born in 1906, making him eighty-one at
the time of his death. His birthplace was given as New York
City, and he had lived there through his thirtieth year, having
attended Columbia University and worked as a reporter on
several New York papers. He had begun as a mystery writer
in 1930 and had written eight novels, regularly published at
a rate of one per year, somewhat in the vein of S.S. Van Dine
and the early Ellery Queen. His sleuth was the traditional
man-about-town amateur detective, in this case called Henry
Friday. In 1936, the modest fame of his books had caused
Wilbur to be offered a Hollywood studio contract and he had
come to the coast to write scripts for a Henry Friday movie
series. DeMarco had never married. His last screen credits
were on a couple of films released in 1938 but shot in 1937.
After that, the books had no information on him.

Articles from the reference books turned up one other salient fact. During his Hollywood stint, Wilbur DeMarco's name had occasionally appeared in the paper in connection with benefits for labor organizations, civil-rights defense funds, support for the loyalists in Spain, and other liberal causes.

"A real show-biz lefty," Stu said over their Wednesday night pizza. "One of those 'premature anti-Fascists.' If he'd still been around fifteen years later, he might have been in big trouble, had his name on the blacklist."

"Do you think he was a Communist?" Rachel said.

"Who knows? Maybe. But you didn't have to be to get in political trouble in fifties Hollywood. A pink necktie would do it."

"The sheriff's men are through with Wilbur's house," Rachel said casually. "And Adam Kane hasn't nailed his young junkie yet."

Stu made a face. "I can't believe you're still thinking of . . ."

"I expect to move in this weekend if I can work things out with Arthur Blemker—that's Wilbur's cousin. I'm going to see him tomorrow morning. He lives out in the Valley."

"You're sure in a hurry."

"I only have two weeks to do this. That's what I'm giving myself, because that's what I can afford. Besides, I want to go up there again for the weekend. For that dance Ernest Basset mentioned."

"Oh, yeah, the Town Prom. I can just see it. A bunch of old musicians who peaked in World War II trying to look and sound like Glenn Miller, and all the locals lurching around the floor with arthritic abandon."

"That's a nice phrase, but a little cruel. Groucho Marx?"
Stu shook his head. "Oscar Levant."

"Whoever said it never went to the Town Prom. Gil says the band is really good. And not everybody in Idyllwild's retirement age, you know. You'll come up with me, won't you?"

"I don't know, Rachel . . ."

"Well, if you don't want to, I could probably scrape up another date."

"Roger, you mean? The old actress's dutiful son? I should abandon you to his attentions. It'd serve you right."

"He's not bad looking, you know."

"Oh, no indeed. You'd make a beautiful couple. I'll bet he's a great conversationalist, too."

"I don't know, but he looks strong. He'd probably be glad to help me move the books back into Wilbur's house."

Stu complacently reached for the last slice of pizza. "Rachel, I know you too well. You want no part of that guy."

"You take a lot for granted, don't you?" Rachel refilled their wine glasses, matching Stu's exaggerated nonchalance with an effort. She had a feeling he would blink first, and she was right.

"How do we dress for this thing?"

"Any way you want, really. They say old prom clothes if you've got 'em."

"No, and I'm not renting any tux. A jacket and tie should be formal enough up there. Do you have your old prom dress?"

"Of course not."

"Do you have a dress?"

Rachel widened her eyes. "Can't I just wear my good jeans?"

"Nope. If I have to sit through a couple hours of big-band music, I at least want a couple of good legs to ogle."

"Who says you're going to sit? You'll be too busy dancing."

"There's not a whole lot I can tell you about Wilbur," said Arthur Blemker. "I never saw much of him after we were kids, and he was a few years older than me, so we weren't very close even then."

DeMarco's cousin was a large, stooped man whose loose skin suggested he had once been much heavier. The

42

vegetable drink he'd offered, a health-food concoction just mixed in his blender, was an odd greenish color, but Rachel rather liked the taste of it. The bookshelves in the living room showed Blemker shared his cousin's literary interests, but the books were far more miscellaneous in condition and value, an accumulation more than a collection. One shelf held a complete set of the eight Henry Friday novels, though in shabby, jacketless copies.

Following Rachel's eyes, Blemker said, "Oh, I liked his books. Still do. I was sorry he quit writing them."

"Do you know why he did?"

"Never could figure it out."

"I think the last one was published in 1937."

"I believe you're right. *Murder Threw Friday.* Not one of the better ones. Too much distraction, I guess, Hollywood and politics. I was never political like Wilbur. I had a job all through the '30s and concentrated on keeping it. It was the people who were out of work and the ones with money and security who could afford to be political."

Rachel doubted that but didn't think it was wise to argue. "Do you know what happened to Wilbur in 1937?"

"Why are you interested?"

"I'm just a kind of '30s buff, I guess." Rachel tried to look guileless. "That's why I want to do this article I'm working on."

"Well, Rachel, early in '38, Wilbur quit Hollywood, quit politics, quit mystery writing, quit most everything. Not much loss, except the mystery writing. I have no idea why he sort of dropped out, like they'd say today, and I've often wondered. Like I told you, we were cordial, exchanged Christmas cards and stuff, but we weren't close. Got news of each other through relatives mostly. Gradually all the relatives died off, which is why I inherit, I guess."

"Didn't Mr. DeMarco ever marry?"

Blemker shook his head. "Nope. That surprised me, too. Wilbur was real attractive to women, and he was crazy about them. Had to fight them off sometimes—I remember he told me once there was a gal worked for his publisher that wanted more than a professional relationship. And he must have had his pick in Hollywood."

"What did he do for a living after he quit writing?"

"During the war he dropped bombs for a living. Other than that, I don't know that he held any job at all. He'd made some lucky investments, and socialist or not, he didn't give all his money away to the masses. I understand he left me a bundle, and if I don't look excited, it's because I already have all the money I can use. Never did have expensive tastes."

"When did he move up to Idyllwild?"

"Only about ten years ago. I saw him once shortly before he moved, and I thought he was interested in something besides the clean mountain air. Secretive, mysterious Wilbur, but what would you expect from a guy who wrote stuff like this?" He gestured toward the bookshelf.

"Can I have a look?" Rachel asked.

"Be my guest."

Rachel pulled off the copy of *Murder Threw Friday*. It was well worn, and the front hinge was broken. On the front flyleaf was a handwritten message:

> February 23, 1937
>
> To Cousin Arthur,
> who likes to escape reality with books like this,
> Revolutionary regards,
> Wilbur DeMarco
> Hollywood, California

"Interesting inscription."

"Peculiar, you mean. We weren't close, as I say, but Wilbur always gave me a copy of his new books, because he knew I liked 'em. Always a little political needle there. At least Wilbur had a sense of humor about his politics, which I think must have kept him from becoming a real card-carrying Commie, don't you?"

44

Rachel didn't answer, but looked at the books somewhat disapprovingly. "You know, if you'd kept these in good condition . . ."

"Sure, sure, scold me. I know how you book dealers think. In dollar signs. But as far as I'm concerned, books were meant to be read. I've read all these half a dozen times and loaned 'em out to friends I don't know how many times. I always threw away the dust jackets. And if there's no bookmark handy, I dog-ear the page I'm on."

Rachel cringed. "Please, say no more."

Arthur Blemker grinned. "I'm not so bad, you know. It's not as bad as clubbing baby seals, is it?"

Rachel managed to grin back. "Of course it isn't. And you're right. Books were meant to be read. Do you think you'd be willing to loan these out one more time? I'd like to read some of Mr. DeMarco's works while I'm living in his house."

"Little morbid, isn't it? Old guy dies like that and you . . ."

"I'm just interested in the past, Mr. Blemker, and I'm not superstitious. I'm practically immune to atmosphere." That was her biggest lie of the morning.

"Young lady, you remind me very much of my cousin Wilbur. Prettier, but every bit as mysterious. Sure, take the books. I'll need them back, though. It's about time to read them again."

"You said you saw Mr. DeMarco when he first moved to Idyllwild. Had you seen him since?"

"Only once, about three years ago. That time Wilbur came to consult me professionally."

"Professionally?"

"My profession. Till I retired, I was a car dealer. More of a car broker, actually. I didn't have a lot or anything, but I kind of brought buyers and sellers together. The last few years, I've been dealing mostly in classic cars. Now it's mostly a hobby, but it can be a lucrative one from time to time. I helped Wilbur get that Duesenberg he had up there. He called me once and told me to watch for any Duesenbergs that came on the market, said he might like one. I told him they were mighty expensive, but he didn't care."

"Why do you think he wanted a Duesenberg particularly?"

"My theory was he wanted one because Ellery Queen drove one, but when I told him that, he just snorted at me. Anyway, I did find a few their owners could be persuaded to part with and invited him down to have a look. When he saw the one he bought, he didn't hesitate, said he couldn't believe his luck. Paid more than the thing was worth, in my opinion, though that was quite a car, I have to admit. Greatest luxury car ever made in the United States."

"I thought the Duesenberg was a German car."

Blemker shook his head emphatically. "No such thing."

"I understand Mr. DeMarco sold the car a couple of weeks before he died."

"I believe that's right."

"Do you know who he sold it to?"

"Not offhand. He didn't use me to broker it, I can tell you that. There's probably a record of it in the financial files we took out of his house. Why do you want to know?"

"Just curious to know why he sold it ahead of everything else, that's all."

"I see. Well, I'll try to find out and tell you. How much was the estate going to charge you to rent the house for two weeks?"

"We hadn't discussed it."

"Well, I guess the estate is me, and I'll settle for a dollar a week. On one condition, that is."

"What's that?"

"When it's all over, you tell me why you *really* wanted to spend time in Wilbur's house. I have a feeling it's the kind of story I'd like."

46

5

THE TOWN PROM band was seven pieces strong, and good. As promised, their repertoire had a mid-century cutoff date and did not encompass anything resembling rock. But Rachel and Stu were not the youngest people there, as they'd feared, and all ages were represented on the small dance floor. Even the band had a couple of members under fifty.

In the middle of one set, Rachel and Stu made their way back to the table they shared with Gil Franklin and a few other local senior citizens. Rachel was limping slightly.

"Out of action already?" Gil said. "Don't you young folks know how to stay in shape?"

Rachel grinned ruefully. "Wounded. That blonde who's dancing with Jud Crompton scored a direct hit on my big toe." She dropped into her chair to inspect the damage.

Stu was looking apologetic. "If I really knew how to dance, I could keep you out of danger."

"Not from those two. There's a pair like that on every dance floor."

Crompton and his partner appeared to be in a world all their own, convinced they were Fred and Ginger, oblivious to the danger they presented other dancers with their elaborate spins and dips and inappropriate changes of direction. By the time they were done with "In the Mood," most of the other dancers were out of it.

The blonde was probably close to Crompton's age and undeniably attractive, but everything about her—hairstyle, dress, and gushy, adolescent manner—was incongruously young enough to make her look faintly ridiculous. To everyone but the fawning Crompton, that is.

"Who is she?" Rachel asked.

"Her name's Alice Zimmer. Runs a gift and crafts shop. Her mom's a bigshot in L.A. society, but Alice prefers the quiet life up here. She and Crompton have been quite an item for some time now." Gil chuckled. "Some folks are making book on how long it will last."

Another number ended. Jud and Alice looked at each other, eyes and teeth gleaming in self-congratulation, while nearly all the other couples fled the floor and a new team of victims took their place.

"It'll last forever," Rachel said. "They're obviously made for each other."

Gil leaned across the table and said confidentially, "Not if Alice finds out what Jud's been up to."

"What's that?"

"This is all just rumor, you understand, but I hear Jud is in the middle of a deal to build houses on Meditation Point."

"You mean where you took us last week? Where everybody goes to see the sunset? But I assumed that was National Forest land."

"Nope. It's privately owned. And I hear Crompton and some associates are putting pressure on the owners to open it up for development. Alice Zimmer's a conservationist and a half, and if she ever found out Jud was working on cutting off access to that view, well, it wouldn't matter how good a dancing partner he was."

Ernest Basset had returned to their table with Dorie Moss, helping the woman to her chair with a courtly manner. "I think I wore out another partner," he said.

"You certainly did," said Dorie. "I like to make a token appearance, but now I think I'll just listen to the music."

"You're not any older than me, Dorie."

"But you're a pro, Ernest. You should be dancing with the younger women."

"Rachel, then." Ernest extended his hand. "How about

it?"

"Go on," Gil Franklin said. "Show Jud and Alice how it's really done."

Rachel shook her head. "Let me take a rain check, Ernest. I need to find the ladies' room and apply some first aid to this toe. I don't know if I want to venture out on that floor again until Torvill and Dean have worn themselves out anyway."

Ernest gave a snort of laughter, and Gil said, "I'm afraid the band will have gone home by then."

But by the time Rachel had threaded her way through the crowd to the door and, after a couple of false turns, found the rest room, reached by a separate outside door, she discovered that even dynamos like Jud and Alice took occasional breaks for bodily functions. The blond gift-shop proprietor was standing in the ladies' room admiring herself in the mirror. Even with her stomach sucked in, she had too much of a spare tire for the skin-tight white dress she was wearing, but she seemed to approve of what she saw. Rachel had to admit that her legs were well molded enough to justify the dress's above-the-knee hem.

Alice looked up as Rachel entered and smiled without recognition. "Hi. Having a good time?"

"Sure," Rachel said. She peeled off her black panty hose to expose the wounded digit and wet a paper towel to wash off the blood.

Alice looked at the toe and said, "Isn't that a shame?"

"Not as bad as it looks. It'll be fine."

"But those hose are ruined. Some of these men just can't stay off your feet, can they?"

Rachel bit back a retort. Couldn't the woman see the spiked heel of her shoe practically imprinted on the toe? Maybe by engaging the blond menace in conversation, she could make a dance or two safe for everybody else.

"Have you been to one of these before?" she asked. "This is my first. I'm new in town."

"Thought I didn't recognize you. I'm Alice Zimmer. I run

49

the Puttering and Pans shop."

"Oh, yes, I've gone by it. I'm Rachel Hennings."

"You permanent or . . ."

"No, just visiting. I'm staying at the Wilbur DeMarco house."

"Oh." A cloud passed over the girlishly middle-aged face. "Why'd you want to do that? That was really sad, wasn't it? It's a nice little house, though." Rachel was glad Alice Zimmer didn't pause for answers to her own questions, determinedly denying any intrusion of reality. "I love things like this dance, I really do. That big-band sound, that's for me. Can't stand rock music, can you? Of course, you're a little younger than I am."

Not more than twenty years, Rachel thought. Talking to this woman, she'd be constantly biting her tongue.

"So few men can dance to this kind of music any more," Alice went on.

"Do you know Ernest Basset?"

"Well, he has a natural advantage, doesn't he? Actually, I meant *young* men. I'm lucky to have Jud. You must have noticed him."

"Oh, yes. I think we've met."

"Well, leave him alone, honey. He's mine, all mine." She seemed to be only half-kidding. "Come by the shop some time, and we'll have some girl talk. No time to talk at an event like this. I love that music so much, I resent having to stop for a pee." She looked back at the mirror and smoothed the white dress over her abdomen a few times. Rachel wanted to tell her it didn't help; her belly was still there. But there was no point in making enemies.

When Alice had left with a coy wave to return to the fray, Rachel took a Band-Aid from her purse, applied it to the toe, and pulled the black pantyhose back on. She regarded the result without enthusiasm. All effect of elegance was gone now with white skin and a Band-Aid exposed through the hole in the toe. But she wasn't vain enough to think very many people were spending the evening fixated on her feet, so she started back for more action, looking forward to a dance with the "naturally advantaged" Ernest Basset.

Before she could get back inside the building, a voice said, "Well, hi there," and a large masculine form appeared out of the shadows.

"Oh, hello," Rachel said, trying to be impersonal but not unfriendly.

"I don't know if you remember me. I'm Roger Payne."

"Yes, of course, how are you?"

"Real fine." The man who'd been memorably handsome in shorts and sweatshirt cut an even more striking figure in a three-piece suit. "Didn't ever expect to see you again. I thought you were a visiting flatlander."

"I am, but I came up to do a little more visiting."

"I hope you're being made welcome."

"People are very friendly up here."

"You're sure looking pretty. You really caught my eye the other day, sad though the occasion was. You were a traffic-stopper in jeans, but this way—well, it's almost more than I can take."

Roger Payne's eyes—at least they weren't staring at the rent toe of her hose—were taking in every detail of her, and she had the uncomfortable feeling he was seeing things he shouldn't. Some eyes are like that.

"How long do you figure to be up here?" he asked.

"Well, it's like this—" To avoid any more personal conversation, she told him about her article and its emphasis on 1937. He listened with stolid attentiveness.

"You'll have to talk to my mom. She was in pictures back then. Frances Payne."

"Oh, of course," Rachel said. "She was famous. Is she here tonight?"

Roger shook his head. "She doesn't get out much. Kind of a recluse, I guess you'd say."

"Would she be willing to talk to me?"

"It might be a little hard to convince her. But with me helping you out, I think we could bring her around." He smiled, and Rachel had to admit the effect was dazzling, in an impersonal sort of way. "It's a little cold out here, isn't it? How about we go inside for a little dance? I suppose this kind of music is as boring for you as it is for me, but old-fashioned dancing has its advantages."

"I really ought to get back to my table."

"I guess you have a date, huh? I came stag myself. Not many of the women up here really interest me. Who you with, a local?"

"Does it matter?" She felt herself getting testy and tried to squelch it. She really did want to talk to Frances Payne—with her Hollywood connection, she might actually have known Wilbur DeMarco in 1937.

"No, no, it's none of my business, but . . . Is it that guy you were with last week? The guy with the beak?"

The insult to Stu made her flare up unrestrainedly. "Look, Adonis, not everybody can look like Tom Selleck, but some people have some manners to go with their . . ."

He smiled again. "With their what? Come on, you started good, now finish it."

"To go with their bottomless chin dimples. Studies show that guys with holes in their chins have holes in their brains."

"Terrific! I do have some manners, and I'll prove it to you. I apologize. Okay?"

She managed to smile back. "Okay. Me, too. I overreacted. And I *would* like to talk to your mother."

"May I see you back to your table? We can dance our way or not, as you prefer."

"Let's walk."

At their table, Roger was all charm chatting with the others, but Stu looked at him balefully. Rachel didn't mind stoking the reporter's jealousy a bit—she was hoping she would at least have him up here weekends during her research, and it didn't hurt to give him an extra incentive.

Jack Hooper, the athletic man who had been among the group outside DeMarco's house the morning the body was found, had joined the others at Rachel's table and launched into an account of a seniors' track meet in which he'd competed in a sprint against Senator Alan Cranston. It was an entertaining story, but Rachel wanted to bring the focus of the conversation back to the '30s.

"Were you a sprinter in the Olympics, too?" she asked.

"Nope. Middle-distance man, eight hundred and fifteen hundred meters. Nowadays, I'm kinda versatile—I run in whatever event is short of competitors. Our old-timers' sprints won't exactly make you forget Carl Lewis, but the senator and I are pretty quick for our age."

"How did you do in the Olympics?" Stu asked.

"I didn't win any medals, but I ran a couple of pretty good races. And I got one close-up in Leni Riefenstahl's documentary," he added with a smirk.

"You're such a perfect Aryan specimen," Gil Franklin said.

"That wasn't the only picture you were in," said Ernest Basset.

Jack looked faintly embarrassed. "Maybe it should have been."

"You were in movies, too?" Rachel said.

"Oh, Hollywood was always looking for athletes to sign to picture contracts in those days."

"*Pretty* athletes," said Ernest.

"I don't know about that. Ones who could act, or learn how, might have pretty good careers. Like Herman Brix, who later changed his name to Bruce Bennett. Those of us who couldn't act, like me, well, we had a little fun and made a little money before they dropped us."

"You could make it even if you couldn't act if they let you play Tarzan," Ernest pointed out.

"Yeah, I think I could have handled Tarzan. But Glen Morris, the decathlon champ, got that job. Really, I kinda think Tarzan *should* have gone to a gold medalist, don't you? It's only fair."

Ernest Basset's eyes were gleaming mischievously. "Maybe they should have given Jesse Owens a shot at Tarzan. Wouldn't a black Tarzan have been something? And it would have saved him racing against horses and all the other things he had to do to make a buck."

Rachel said to Jack, "I suppose you were in Hollywood in 1937."

"Oh, sure. That was my one full year as a movie actor."

"Did you know Wilbur DeMarco then?"

"No, we never met back then. I knew him up here, of course. Wilbur was a heck of a nice guy."

The mention of DeMarco brought conversation to a halt. Breaking the uncomfortable silence, Rachel said, "I don't know if Gil told you, but I'm doing an article, just with Idyllwild people and just about the year 1937. It will be a sort of memorial to Mr. DeMarco, since he collected 1937 things."

"Always wondered why he did that," Jack Hooper said.

"I hope you'll let me interview you one day in the next couple of weeks. Get your memories of that year."

"Even though I didn't know Wilbur then?" Hooper seemed uncomfortable with the idea.

"But it's not about Wilbur. Not really. It's just about that year, what life was like then."

"In Hollywood?"

"All over. Though there do seem to be quite a few people up here who were in the movie industry then."

"It's sort of a local tradition, the Hollywood connection," said Gil. "Marjorie Main had a place up here at one time. So did Charles Laughton and Elsa Lanchester. Also, Mary Pickford and Buddy Rogers did some of their courting on the hill, and Joe DiMaggio and Marilyn Monroe spent some time up here on their honeymoon. Who knows? Maybe if they'd stayed, she'd be alive and they'd still be happily married."

"Things aren't usually that simple," Jack Hooper said.

54

Then he said to Rachel, "Sure, I'll be glad to help you. It'll be kinda fun."

Gil whipped out a pocket-sized spiral notebook and said, "You can arrange your appointment with Ms. Hennings's secretary. When's a good day for you, Jack?"

Rachel was pleased Gil was getting into the spirit of things and taking charge of her interview schedule. For one thing, it was making it clear to everyone that someone else was going to know whom she was talking to on any given day, just in case there really was an elderly murderer lurking in the shadows . . .

"How about that dance now, Rachel?" Ernest Basset said.

She looked toward the dance floor and saw, miraculously, that the tireless Jud and Alice were walking off. "Wonderful timing, Ernest. What was the main dance craze in 1937?"

"Thing called the 'Big Apple' as I recall. Jitterbug step. But we better not try it here, or they'll be calling us Jud and Alice II."

A few hours after the end of the Town Prom, Rachel and Stu stood in the living room of the DeMarco house and looked around at the remnants of 1937. Wilbur's books were all back on the shelves. They had discovered the cache of old radio cassettes and had a vintage "Fibber McGee and Molly" program ready to play when the urge struck them. Rachel had carefully arranged a reconstruction of Wilbur's cryptic mantelpiece display—Stu had found acceptable substitutes for the peanut can, Astor Hotel key, model '37 Chevrolet and the Criterion Theatre ticket stub. She was sure the disappearance of the original objects meant they had some special significance.

"How does that look?" she asked.

"Close enough," Stu said judiciously. "Not quite like the original items, though. I want you to know it took a lot of work to gather those duplicates, and I hope it doesn't spoil your mystical emanations that they're phony. The peanut can is

'40s vintage, and the tickets and hotel key are '87 bogus."

"They're real enough for the effect I want. I just want people to see them. If they don't notice, I'll make sure to call their attention to the things there."

"Oh, yeah," Stu grumbled. "I can't believe you want to go through with this."

"I can hardly turn back now. Gil's got a full appointment book for me."

"He's senile. What's your excuse?"

"You know he isn't senile. Stu, you're lousy company tonight."

"Sorry. Maybe I should just drive down the hill right now. You'll have to get used to sleeping in this museum by yourself soon enough anyway."

"I don't want you to go, Stu. But I wish you'd lighten up a little bit."

"Lighten up, huh? In an isolated house where a murder was committed a week ago and where you're lining up a series of afternoon teas hoping to entertain the murderer. I know you like the company of ghosts, Rachel, but at least the ghosts in Vermilion's are friendly ones."

"Are you trying to scare me, by any chance?"

"If I thought I could do that, I wouldn't be so damned frustrated. I might as well try to spook Refrigerator Perry with a fright wig as scare any sense into you."

Rachel put her arms around his waist. "You overestimate my intrepidness, Stu. This place is scarier at night than in the daytime, and I'm thankful you're here to protect me."

"Don't kid me," Stu said, but his voice was softening. "Your helpless-little-me act couldn't be less convincing if you were Gloria Steinem."

"Well, that's an improvement over Refrigerator Perry anyway."

Stu laughed in spite of himself and pulled her closer to him. They held each other for a moment before Rachel pushed him away gently.

56

"There's something I'd like you to do for me when you get back to Los Angeles tomorrow."

"What's that?"

"Call Arthur Blemker, Wilbur's cousin. Tell him I asked you to call and get the name of the classic-car collector in Newport Beach Wilbur sold his Duesenberg to. Then Monday or Tuesday go talk to the buyer and see if Wilbur said anything to him that might help us."

Stu was exasperated. "And what might that be?"

"I don't know, but there could be something. And there must have been some reason Wilbur decided to get rid of the car a couple weeks before everything else."

"There must, huh?"

"I thought you liked old cars, Stu."

"I do, but Newport Beach is not Los Angeles . . . I have to work for a living, you know."

"Do an article about it for the paper. The *News-Canvass* doesn't have an Orange County bureau."

Stu sighed. "People have the funniest ideas about reporters. Think freedom of the press means you don't have a boss. All right, I'll do what I can."

Rachel grinned. "Thanks. Now I have a surprise for you. While you were working on my fireplace exhibit, I was acquiring a full 1937 wardrobe, authentic from the skin out."

"Really? Garter belt and the whole bit?"

"Yes. Want me to put it on for you?"

"I'd rather you took it off for me actually."

"But to do that, I'll have to put it on first, won't I? You turn on 'Fibber McGee and Molly' and I'll be right back."

Stu watched her walk out of the room, admiringly as always. Then he noticed that an old *Life* magazine on the coffee table was open to an illustrated article called "How to Undress for Your Husband." The old picture mag could get surprisingly risqué in those days. Stu thumbed the pages, comparing the plumpish 1937 bodies with Rachel's sleeker 1987 model. Wishing he could stay all week, he completely forgot to turn on "Fibber and Molly."

When Rachel appeared again, she certainly looked as if she'd stepped out of a Depression-era magazine, but her appearance wasn't the least bit depressing. She wore a form-fitting grey suit with vertical stripes, belted at the waist.

"Like it?" she said.

"Sure. But what makes it 1937 exactly?"

"The skirt length for one thing." It came to mid-calf.

"A pity. The one bad point. Why'd they have to make Depression times more depressing with those long skirts?"

In a fashion-commentator voice, Rachel said, "Note also the stitched-down pleats and the slight flare at the knee."

"I'd rather notice the knee."

"The jacket comes hip-length, and there is just a suggestion of padding at the shoulders. This is a felt hat—note the long black feather. Note, too, the practical but attractive low-heeled walking shoes. The fur is fox."

"You look sensational," Stu said. "Almost enough to make me want to be a time-traveler. Don't like that fur, though."

"Kind of gross, isn't it?" she agreed, looking distastefully at the intact head and paws and slipping it off her shoulders. "You know how I feel about animal furs, but this guy's been dead for a long time."

Stu gestured to the magazine. "That's some article."

She nodded. "They got letters about that. Corrupting innocent youth, putting prurient thoughts in their heads."

"How about putting some in my head."

Rachel lay the fox fur over a chair and her hands went to the top button of her suit. Then she looked at Stu with feigned shock. "But you're not my husband!"

"This isn't 1937, either."

6

ON MONDAY MORNING, Rachel was munching a piece of toast, savoring a cup of coffee, and enjoying the cunningly arranged view from Wilbur DeMarco's small dining room table. Tall trees, hills, no other houses, and only an occasional glimpse of winding road to suggest the incursion of civilization. There were antique Huggins Young and G. Washington cans on the bar, but the coffee in the cup was Taster's Choice. The toast from the still-working 1937 toaster didn't really seem so extraordinary, but probably there was a difference between today's bread and the bread of fifty years ago. She could glance at the headlines of a '37 newspaper with her breakfast, but there was no way she could eat '37 food. Much as she tried to imagine herself a Jack Finney character, no spontaneous time-travel was taking place.

Stu had returned to the city late Sunday afternoon, looking as worried as ever. She was almost disappointed at the lack of terror in her first night alone in the house. She had listened to some old radio shows, read one of the Henry Friday novels straight through, and gone to sleep immediately. The quiet of the mountains was taking no getting used to. She had been awakened earlier than planned, though, by the noise of a woodpecker assaulting the side of the house.

Gil had scheduled her first interview for 10 A.M., but she heard a car stopping in front of the drive a half hour before that. The unexpected visitor was Deputy Adam Kane, looking very uneasy.

"Miss Hennings, I'm a little puzzled," he said.

"About what?"

"What you're doing here, living in this house. It's uh, kind of unusual."

"I understood the sheriff's department had okayed the house being rented."

"Well, we're through with it as a crime scene, but . . ."

"I don't understand what's troubling you, Deputy."

"You're a young woman living alone in a house where a murder's been committed."

"That's true. Do you have some reason to think I'm in danger?"

"Well, no, not really, but . . ."

"Mr. DeMarco was either killed by a youth looking for drugs, as you think, or he was killed for some personal motive. Either way, that doesn't endanger me, does it?"

"No, not necessarily, and it's up to you what you do, Miss Hennings. I just wanted to—to come by and say hello."

"Hello, then. I can assure you all the locks are working just fine, and I don't plan on letting in any wandering drug addicts."

"I'm sure you don't but—Miss Hennings, it's just not natural, that's all."

"I wanted a place to live while I visit up here for a couple of weeks. What could be more natural than that? I also want to work on a magazine article in honor of the late Mr. DeMarco, and what better location could I have to do it? And if you need any more information from me, I'll be handy."

Kane was clearly annoyed, but he obviously didn't know what to say. "I doubt that I will, Miss Hennings, but I appreciate your making yourself available."

"Thanks for coming by, Mr. Kane," Rachel said, smiling. "And I'm sorry if I seemed ungrateful for your interest. Will you do me one favor?"

"Sure, if I can."

"When you locate the kid or kids who burgled this house looking for drugs, will you let me know? It will make the rest of my work here a good deal more enjoyable if you do."

"I certainly will. Have a nice day." Adam Kane fumed his way down the path, and Rachel hoped she hadn't antagonized him. At some point, she might have to convince him of something, and it wouldn't help to make him an enemy.

Promptly on the hour, Gil Franklin delivered Dorie Moss to her door. Invited to stay, he declined. "You'll do your best work one-on-one, Rachel. I don't want to be influenced by anyone else's reminiscences when I get around to regaling you with my own memories. You just got a sample the other day."

"Well, come back at noon and join us for lunch," Rachel insisted.

"Oh, we musn't stay for lunch," Dorie said.

"It's the least I can do. And it's all made, just needs heating up."

"Too bad Wilbur didn't have a microwave," Gil said.

Rachel admonished him jokingly. "Don't mention such modern contrivances. I'm trying to live in the past here."

"At our age, that can be dangerous, eh, Dorie?"

"Oh, I don't think a couple of hours will hurt."

When Gil had left, Dorie Moss stood for a moment looking around Wilbur's living room. Rachel invited her to sit down, but she was distressed to see the older woman's eyes had filled with tears.

"Do we have to talk in here?" she said. "Couldn't we go out on the deck?"

"Won't you be cold?"

"Certainly not. I don't think I can talk about things in here. Things just loom up . . ."

Did she mean the finding of Wilbur's body or something else? At any rate, Rachel had no desire to cause the older woman pain, and she readily agreed to move the operation to the deck, overlooking the trees below. Conditions for recording their conversation on her cassette recorder were less than ideal, but Dorie seemed much happier.

"I'm sorry I started to get emotional in there," she said with a rueful smile, "but I spent quite a bit of time in that room with Wilbur. I might as well tell you before somebody else does that I was very, very fond of Wilbur, not just as a friend. I often thought I might become his wife one day, though I don't know if he'd ever have gotten around to asking. Guess you think the whole idea'd be silly at our age . . ."

"No, not at all."

"Some folks our age think so, though. In fact, I think a lot of people thought I was shamelessly chasing after Wilbur. Very undignified, but I don't care. I'm too old to worry about dignity. Never did much when I was young, come to think of it." She looked at the recorder. "I'm well known locally for talking too much. I'm not talking about my love life when you turn that thing on, though."

Rachel smiled. "I just want to talk about 1937." She raised her pad of yellow paper. "I have my questions all ready. Did you know Mr. DeMarco in those days, Dorie?"

"Oh, no, certainly not. I didn't live in this part of the country then. I was a Midwestern girl, lived in a little town in Iowa . . ."

Rachel raised her hand. "Wait. Before we start, I have to be sure I can pick you up out here." She switched on the recorder. "Just say something in a normal tone of voice."

"Well, uh, you might see a quail family or two from this deck pretty soon. It's almost the time of year for the little ones to be born."

Rachel stopped the recorder, rewound, and played back Dorie's words. The older woman made a face.

"Last time I heard my voice recorded was on my Uncle Jim's wire recorder just after the war. I hated the sound of it then, and it's even worse now."

"Everybody feels that way. I hate listening to myself, too."

"But you have a lovely voice. I sound like a little old lady. Of course, I *am* a little old lady, but who wants reminders?"

"Just talk and don't worry about it." Rachel started up the

recorder again, saying the date and the name of her subject. Then she asked, "Where were you living in 1937, Dorie?"

Dorie's story of a small-town youth in Iowa was interesting enough, but only one aspect of it had any apparent connection with Wilbur DeMarco's activities at the same time. She had been a bit of a union activist, which had scandalized her conservative family, had even tried to organize a sit-down strike in the drugstore where she worked.

"Did Wilbur DeMarco ever talk to you about his union activities in the '30s?"

"Oh, a little bit. I mean, we talked about his opinions, and I knew he was a supporter of labor by what he said. Fellow lefties, I guess that's what made us kindred spirits, huh? But did he have something directly to do with unions?"

"So I understand, at least in raising funds to support them."

"Well, I'll be darned. I never knew that. We would talk about 1937, of course, in a general way—we were bound to, with that collection of his surrounding us—but not about what he was doing himself then. Or what I was doing, come to think of it. Wilbur never talked much about himself. I didn't even know he'd been a writer till you and Gil told me."

"Did you and he talk about local issues affecting Idyllwild?"

Dorie was beginning to look suspicious. "Rachel, I get the impression you're interested in something besides 1937 here."

Rachel switched off the recorder. "Sorry, I guess I'm just not a very professional interviewer. I wander around too much. The subject is allowed to do that, of course, but the interviewer is supposed to keep to the subject."

"It's okay. I don't mind. Like most people up here, Wilbur wanted to be the last newcomer, didn't want to see any more growth or any more inroads of development. We all feel that way, losing battle or not."

"Did Wilbur have enemies in town?"

"No," Dorie said sharply. "I mean, if he did, I didn't know of any. He kept mostly to himself, and everything he ever did for the community was positive. And of course, he was valued as a colorful local character. Takes one to know one, huh?"

"Then who do you think killed him?"

"I thought that was a kid looking for drugs. Didn't Adam Kane say . . . ?"

"That's the police theory. Do you agree with it?"

"I have no choice. Why'd anyone want to kill Wilbur for a personal reason? It's a silly idea."

"Well, you said he opposed development."

"Sure he opposed it. But he never did anything about it, to the extent of even writing a letter to the *Town Crier*. Rachel, Wilbur lived in a world of his own, a world none of us could really penetrate. Certainly not me. I can assure you he created no motives for murder among the people in Idyllwild. And I think I'd know if he did. I knew him as well as anybody up here, though nowhere near as well as I'd've liked."

"Ever have a ride in his Duesenberg?"

Dorie looked at her oddly. "No, I didn't. He was kind of funny about that car. He'd use it for errands in town, but I don't think he liked it very much."

"He didn't like it?"

"That's what I thought. Sounds funny, doesn't it, the money he must have paid for it?"

"Did he say why?"

"Never said a thing. It's just a feeling I had, that's all."

Rachel looked at her watch. "Gil won't be back for another hour or so, and lunch won't take more than fifteen minutes to put together. Shall we talk a little more for the record?"

She switched the recorder back on, and Dorie added some reminiscences of life in 1937. When they finally went back inside, Rachel drew Dorie's attention to the display on the

64

mantelpiece.

"Did Wilbur ever explain to you what all that meant?" Rachel asked.

Dorie peered at the four objects. "Never saw these things before."

"They weren't always here?"

"No. Last time I was here before the morning ... it happened ... was maybe a month ago, and these weren't here then."

"Any idea what they might mean?"

"Uncle of mine had a car pretty much like that one before the war. I've eaten a few Planter's Peanuts in my time, but I've never been to the Hotel Astor or the Criterion Theatre. Unless it was one in Des Moines. Never been to New York at all. This means nothing to me, Rachel."

But, Rachel told herself, if the vanishing mantel exhibit was a recent addition, she was surer than ever that it meant something to somebody.

7

STU HAD SPENT a pleasurable morning looking at more vintage cars than he had ever seen outside of a museum while listening to a tireless lecture by their enthusiastic owner. Once Arthur Blemker had told him the name of the Duesenberg's buyer, Dwight Purvis, associations began to click. In that pile of review copies on his desk was a new book on classic American automobiles, and the author was the very same Dwight Purvis of Newport Beach. With a considerable effort, Stu managed to convince a dubious editor a feature article on Purvis and his collection should accompany his review.

Purvis was a smallish man in his forties who spoke in a harsh monotone and seemed to have no life or interest outside of his car collection. But he had a story to tell about every classic in his stable, and Stu listened to them all, scribbling a note occasionally to jog his memory. He hadn't mentioned that the last car they came to was the one he was most interested in.

Wilbur DeMarco's Duesenberg was a bright red convertible coupe. It seemed to Stu to be in beautiful condition, but its owner was apologizing for its incomplete restoration.

"Bought it from an old guy up in the hills. He actually drove it around town. The Duesenberg was one of the finest American cars ever produced, but only the rich ever drove one—movie stars, company presidents, people like that. They sold for fourteen to twenty-five grand, and you can imagine what kind of money that was in the Depression. This one sold for seventeen-five, but worth every penny if you had it to spend. It's a model SJN. Rollston of New York designed the body—Duesenberg never built their own bodies. Eight-cylinder engine, 320 horsepower at 4200 RPM. Could do a hundred and four miles per hour in second gear. No telling how fast it could go in high. Fuel tank held twenty-six gallons, standard on a Duesenberg, and they always had those two spare wheels mounted in the fender walls."

Stu waited patiently for the technical details to blow over. They he asked as casually as he could manage, "Who did you say you bought it from?"

"Old guy named Wilbur DeMarco, lived up in Idyllwild."

"DeMarco? Wasn't he the guy who was murdered up there the other day?"

Purvis looked surprised but only mildly interested. "Was he?"

"You hadn't heard?"

"I don't read the papers or watch much TV. These babies are my whole life."

"Did DeMarco say anything about why he wanted to sell it?"

Purvis looked suspicious now. "I thought you wanted to do an article about me and my book and my collection."

"I am, but this is a story, too. You might know something that would have a bearing on DeMarco's death."

"Why haven't the police asked me then?"

"I don't know. Look, Mr. Purvis, I'd be grateful if there was anything you could tell me. I had to fight my editor to get to do this story, and when it appears, it should do you and your book some good. I don't think it's asking too much . . ."

Purvis waved a hand. "Of course it isn't. I'll help any way I can. But I don't really remember anything he said. He just wanted to sell it, and he knew what it was worth. I had to pay the price, you can believe it. Drove it down the hill myself. A nervous drive, I can tell you." Purvis looked nervous now, reliving it.

Stu approached the same question several different ways

and got nothing more about Purvis's dealings with DeMarco. Not so surprising maybe. The car collector didn't strike him as someone who would be very observant of people. Cars really were more alive to him.

When the tour of the collection was over, and Purvis was walking Stu back to his own more-mundane-than-ever Japanese import, Stu asked, "Was 1937 a good year for the Duesenberg?"

Purvis snorted. "Terrible year. Company went belly-up."

"Oh, then DeMarco's car must have been one of the last Duesenbergs, huh?"

Purvis shrugged. "Not really."

"Well, if it was a '37 . . ."

"Who said it was a '37?"

"I thought—"

"Why would you think that? I never said it was a '37. That car's a 1936."

8

RACHEL'S AFTERNOON APPOINTMENT arrived via Gil Franklin's taxi service at two o'clock. His name was Vernon Spiegel, a short, stocky man with a jovial face and a deep, well-modulated voice. He was dressed in a dark suit, more formal than the occasion and the surroundings seemed to warrant.

"Vern's an old radio man, can you tell?" Gil said.

"Yes, I think I recognize your voice," Rachel said.

Spiegel looked pleased. "I do still get some voice-over work occasionally. Not officially retired, though I feel no need to live down in the smog any more."

When Gil had left and they were sitting in the living room, Rachel putting a fresh cassette in her recorder, Spiegel reached into his jacket pocket and pulled out a fistfull of three-by-five-inch cards. Rachel looked at them apprehensively.

"I did a little research," he explained. "I wanted to be well prepared on 1937."

"Oh, that's nice, but . . ."

"Preparation is the key to success in radio. I've done it all—news, disc-jockeying, interviews, sports play-by-play, commercials, even drama. Always well prepared. And in my day, you had a script for almost everything except the play-by-play and *some* of the interviews—there wasn't all this modern emphasis on ad-libbing. What somebody else might call spontaneity, I might call plain sloppiness. Always dressed up for the microphone in those days, too. Not in formal dress like the BBC did, you understand, but still—some people thought it improved the sound if you were well dressed, even if the listener couldn't see it."

"We should get that all on tape," Rachel said. "Let me just get this going and introduce you." She pressed the button, gave her usual introduction with the day's date, and asked, "Mr. Spiegel, what is your most distinct memory of 1937?"

To her dismay, she'd given him just the opening he wanted. In a mellifluous voice, he began reading from the cards a compendium of 1937 facts and statistics. She wanted to stop him and say, no, that's not the point. I want what you remember, not facts out of an almanac. But the material was interesting enough and no waste of tape, so she decided to let it run its course, then try to get some more personal recollections. For several minutes, Spiegel spouted about sports figures—Joe Louis, War Admiral, Don Budge, Alice Marble, and a guy named DiMaggio; political leaders—Neville Chamberlain, Franco, Hitler, Mussolini; literary figures—Faith Baldwin, Max Brand, Maxwell Anderson, Eugene O'Neill.

Rachel suppressed a sigh. All potted history, but she couldn't fault Spiegel's smooth and dramatic delivery.

Finally, with a reference to the U.S.A.'s two million home refrigerators, compared to Britain's three thousand, and the world's largest flower in New York City Botanical Gardens (an eight-and-a-half-foot calla lily with a four-foot diameter and twelve-foot circumference), Spiegel ran out of note cards.

"That was just marvelous," Rachel said. "You really did a job there."

"It was nice to have the excuse actually. I've always liked that kind of thing. Sort of a 'March of Time' feel, don't you think? I've always thought I could do a show like Paul Harvey's 'Rest of the Story,' but I've never been able to interest anybody."

"Actually, though, the point of this memoir is the things you remember firsthand."

70

Spiegel laughed. "I don't remember much of what I just told you, I have to admit. Remember Hitler and his friends, of course, though I didn't know them personally."

"Were you working in radio in 1937?"

"Oh, yes, just starting out, though. I was only twenty-two, but I had my own noon-hour interview show on a station in Oasis Springs, out in the desert. One of my guests on that show was a visiting author named Wilbur DeMarco."

Rachel's reaction was satisfactorily excited. "You knew Wilbur in 1937?"

"I can't say I knew him well, but I did interview him and talked to him some off the air, too."

"You don't have a tape of that interview, do you?"

Spiegel shook his head. "Wish I did, but there was no tape in those days. If anything got recorded, it went on wax, and we didn't usually record much. I'd give a lot to be able to listen to some of that stuff now."

"Can you remember anything about your interview with Wilbur DeMarco?"

"Not a whole lot. I think we talked a little about the history of detective fiction, Poe and Doyle and all that. And we talked about some of the big names at that time—S.S. Van Dine and Mary Roberts Rinehart and Ellery Queen. We talked a little about his current book, and I think I asked him what he thought of the movie version of Henry Friday. On the air, he loved it, but off the air, I got the feeling he was not so enthusiastic. Oh, I think I asked him what he was currently working on, and he said there'd be another Henry Friday book in 1938, but he never discussed the details of work in progress. Spoiled it, he said."

"But he definitely was working on another novel?"

"Oh, yes."

"But it was never published."

"Wasn't it? I can't say I looked for it. I didn't really care for the Henry Friday books. Dashiell Hammett was more my speed."

71

"Did he tell you anything about what he was doing in Hollywood?"

Spiegel shook his head. "Not that I remember. Oh, I'm sure I asked him a bunch of questions off the air, goggle-eyed kid that I was, but nothing about what he was doing personally. He was always a closemouthed type about personal things."

"You knew Wilbur up here, too, though?"

"Oh, certainly."

"Did you ever talk to him about those days, or about your interview with him?"

"I mentioned it to him once, but he didn't remember it at all. He didn't seem to want to talk about his literary career, either—a lot of folks up here didn't even know he was a writer. We wound up conversing on the usual Idyllwild subjects—barking dogs, location of the dump, public rest rooms in town, all that interesting stuff."

Rachel smiled. "I guess I've gotten us off the subject."

"Have you, young lady, or is it really the life story of Wilbur DeMarco you're working on?"

"That's just incidental," she said and to prove it, brought the conversation back to details of life in 1937.

At the end of the interview, when Rachel had snapped off the recorder, Vernon Spiegel looked around the room and said, "It seems a real happy time, looking back. I'm kind of sorry to leave it. I wonder how Wilbur found all this stuff."

"It's not all visible," Rachel said. "Down in the cellar, I found a couple of racks full of 1937-vintage wine."

"No kidding? Not many places up here with cellars. I wonder if he ever drank any."

"Wouldn't it have turned to vinegar by now?"

"Not necessarily. Not in just fifty years. That's if they're red wines anyway. You should try some while you're staying here. Wine was meant to be drunk, after all."

"I'm afraid I'd have to get permission from the estate before I started raiding the cellar. Mr. Spiegel, have you ever visited here before?"

"Never. Very few people did. Dorie Moss, I suppose. They were supposed to be a sort of an item, you know."

"Did you notice the exhibit on the mantel?"

Spiegel turned and looked at it. "Let's see now. I sure do remember that Chevy—there were a lot of them around, of course. The Criterion Theatre and the Astor Hotel were both near Times Square in New York. But what've they got to do with these other things . . . ? You know, I have a feeling I should know the connection, but I can't put my finger on it."

"Think about it, and let me know if you have any ideas. The juxtaposition of items meant something to Wilbur."

At that moment, Gil Franklin hit the doorbell.

"Is my time up?" Spiegel said. "I feel like I just got here."

Rachel opened the door for Gil, who said, "How'd it go, folks? Did old 'Housewives' Protective League' put you to sleep?"

Spiegel rose from his chair to join the good-natured combat. "I was never a Housewives' Protective League guy, Franklin. Couldn't get that folksy, phlegmy voice down."

"What in the world are you two talking about?" Rachel asked.

"Believe me, you don't want to know," Spiegel said. "But if Franklin tells you I was the announcer on 'John's Other Wife' or did the first Ex-Lax commercial, don't listen to him. You come to drive me home, have you? I don't need an ambulance service, you know. I can still navigate for myself."

"I'm part of the Researchers' Protective League, and I'm just doing my job. I know you, Spiegel. If you came on your own, you'd never know when to go home. Besides, I made Rachel another appointment for tonight."

Rachel received the news with mixed feelings. "Tonight? Gil, I thought we were doing two a day."

"Well, this guy's a painter who worships light, so he only schedules nonartistic pursuits after dark."

"Klingsburg, right?" said Spiegel. "What a pain in the ass that old fraud is. Just remember, Rachel, he thinks he's Diego Rivera or something and needs to have his ego stroked constantly. I've interviewed *him* on the radio, too. An indelible memory. You better pretend you've heard of him."

"William Klingsburg, the muralist? Of course, I've heard of him. But I didn't know he lived up here."

"Only part of the time," said Gil. "He has houses all over the place." With a wink, he added, "The 'old fraud' seems to have convinced the world he's a great artist."

"I suppose he's all right," Spiegel said grudgingly. "But I have a nephew who's better by a mile and can't even sell his work."

The three of them walked out to Gil's car in the driveway. After Vernon Spiegel had climbed into the passenger seat, Gil said softly to Rachel, "You'll want to talk to this guy. He not only knew Wilbur in 1937, he knew him damn well. And you've got tomorrow morning off, to sleep in if you want."

"I doubt if the woodpeckers will let me. I'll have a walk into town."

"Good idea. You've got Ernest Basset in the afternoon, Jack Hooper the next morning. I don't think Frances Payne will come to you, but her son Roger thinks she might talk to you if you go there."

"If I have to. But that 1937 room seems to help open people up."

"Well, I've never been to the Paynes', but I have the feeling she's living in the past every bit as much as Wilbur did. I'll be by with Klingsburg around seven-thirty."

"Gil, should you be driving around up here in the dark?"

"Rachel, if you don't do something to quell your ageism—the danger up here isn't from cars. Unless you're a squirrel, of course."

74

9

THE LOGS IN Wilbur DeMarco's fireplace had caught nicely, and the 1937 room was filled with warmth. There were three of them sitting and watching the flames flicker. This time, Rachel had insisted that Gil stay, partly because she worried about his driving the twisty mountain roads at night any more than necessary and partly because William Klingsburg, unlike the open and friendly Dorie Moss and Vernon Spiegel, really did make her a little edgy. He was nearly as tall and thin as Gil, with a still-handsome hawklike profile and thick black eyebrows that contrasted dramatically with the white hair on his head.

"The '30s," he was saying. "We lived in them only ten years, and yet they defined our whole lives."

Not a bad epigram, though Rachel had the feeling he'd been polishing it for years, bringing it out for occasional exhibit like one of his more easily portable paintings.

"I want to hear your memories of 1937, Mr. Klingsburg," she said. "What were you doing in that year?"

"I was painting." Dramatic, tape-wasting pause. "What was I doing in any year but painting and trying to live and eat by what I painted? I traveled many roads and painted many things all through those years. The times were cruel, and I was trying to record them, not cruelly. I had few patrons. The best of them was Mr. Roosevelt with his WPA. Imagine the United States Government encouraging the arts. Would we had that today."

It was like listening to one of those talking figures you see in museums, as if William Klingsburg weren't there at all, just his simulacrum. He spoke with deliberate slowness, choosing his words like colors from his palette. Was there really any hope of getting something useful from this man? Gil had seemed to think so.

"Were you working on a WPA project in 1937?"

"A mural. In Los Angeles. In a post office. They call me Klingsburg the Muralist. That is my tag. Every man must have his tag. Murals were a part of the '30s, and murals are a legitimate expression of people's lives and what they value. But they are not all of art nor all of me. Still, I am pleased with that mural and some others. I brought them light and shadow and depth. Nothing flat about them. But little of my work is in the form of murals, and I haven't attempted one since 1952, when the world was middle-aged. And I paint every day and seek the light. Still, I shall die Klingsburg the Muralist."

"I think I've seen that mural. It's very good."

"Only as good as a mural can be. For I am Klingsburg the Muralist."

Rachel caught Gil's eye for an instant, and she had the feeling they should have laughed at the artist's posturing. But there was nothing funny about it. Was this strange, distant man putting on a well-honed act for them? Was he really there with them at all?

"What was your life like in 1937 aside from the painting?"

"Was there life aside from the painting? Is there ever life aside from the painting? Is anything off the canvas real at all? Yes, I have to say it was. It may not be today, or not for me, but at that time, it was. There was struggle. There is always struggle. But now there is not my struggle. But then there was. Struggle to make the lives of people better. Struggle for ideas that burned bright in our innermost soul. What do I do when I lift my brush or put my hands in the clay? I organize. And what do people do to lift their lives from oppression? Organize! Organize! Where men and women came to organize, I would be there, too." Dramatic pause.

"I never was the life of the party."

It sounded like a witticism, but Klingsburg's face stayed blank as ever, without a trace of humor. "But I was at the party, always at the party. I could not sing the labor songs or play on the guitar. But I could draw a quick sketch, a caricature, to help raise funds from those who had for those who needed. Where men and women came to organize, in barns or warehouses or smoke-filled meeting rooms or Beverly Hills drawing rooms, there came Klingsburg the Muralist."

"And was Wilbur DeMarco there, too?"

For the first time, the barest hint of a smile twitched at the corners of Klingsburg's lips. "Yes, Wilbur DeMarco was there, too. Always."

"Were you friends?"

"I am not a friend. I would not claim to be a friend. Can a man live for art and work for mankind and still have energy to be a friend? Wilbur could be a friend, but he practiced a debased art. It's true that Wilbur worked diligently, one book per annum, as immutable as Christmas or Groundhog Day. Even at those parties, he would slip away, pound his keys, hammer out carpenterlike his 1938 opus. He smiled when he spoke of it, hinted we were all to be characters on his bloody pages.

"Wilbur had time and energy to be a friend. Wilbur could even love. I do think he loved her. An unofficial love, a furtive love, but genuine nonetheless, I always thought."

"Loved whom, Mr. Klingsburg?" Rachel leaned forward; here was something new—and possibly important.

She was sure the painter had heard the question, but he wasn't ready to answer just yet. "I lay with many women in those years. I used and appreciated their bodies, tall and short, thin and well rounded. But never did I love. Never did I claim to love. Could I paint and create and be Klingsburg the Muralist and be able to love, too? I could not be so egotistical. But Wilbur could love. I think that was Wilbur's true art."

Rachel glanced at Gil, who raised his eyebrows. Should she try to prod Klingsburg for details again or just let him run on and hope he would get to the point?

"Wilbur had an odd idea of art. He appreciated overmuch the magazine illustrators. N.C. Wyeth. Norman Rockwell. James Montgomery Flagg. And he cherished motion picture and theatrical posters. He collected them at a time no one else was interested in such transitory abominations. Bad art. Debased art. I had my opportunities to work in that field. Wilbur did his best to convince me that I should. Steady work, he said. Steady. Art is not steady. Art is not one a year. Art is not ready by Thursday. But I was thin and badly clad, and Wilbur meant the best for me. I think he was my friend, even if I could not be his. And I am sure he loved her."

The firelight flickered, and Klingsburg stared straight into it. Rachel decided to try the direct approach once more.

"Whom did he love, Mr. Klingsburg?"

"She was lovely. Women's bodies can be high art, whether the artist is chance or nature or some invisible God the Muralist. I knew many like her who were giantized on screens by the basest art of all, the art of calculated falsification. Few were as lovely as she. Few needed as little the tools of celluloid phoniness as she. Gladly would I have fondled those proud breasts. But she had a husband she hated and a Wilbur DeMarco to love, though not openly, not officially. I had no hope to see her body bare, to get inside her. I could not even ask to paint her nude, for I painted no nudes, and I could not dissemble. My beddings were direct, and I think appreciated."

"Who is the woman you're talking about, Mr. Klingsburg? A movie star?"

He didn't answer right away but gave the question careful consideration. "She may have had star billing. But was she truly a star? Or did she have too much conscience, too much intelligence, too much essential beauty? I slept with women who were far bigger stars than she, but they did not have what she had. Had they had it, they could not have been such trivial things as stars."

Almost despairing of getting an actual name from the painter, Rachel decided to play a hunch. "Was her name by any chance Frances Payne?"

An astonishing thing happened. Klingsburg laughed, an openmouthed roar that lasted only a second but left Rachel with a cold chill, despite the warmth from the fireplace. She was sure Gil felt it, too, but she was glad she'd talked him into staying.

"An inadvertent insult to her memory. No, not Frances Payne, no indeed. No, the name of Wilbur's love, my lust, was Sally Jordan. Surely I mentioned her name before."

"You know you didn't," Gil said. "You plan your conversations as carefully as your paintings."

Ignoring the jibe, Klingsburg said, "I think you'll find traces of Sally all over the record of Wilbur's life, the record he's left in this house. Posters probably, the art of the lobbies. But they never did her justice. A great artist might, but not a commercial poster artist."

"There are some posters," Rachel said. "In his bedroom closet, but I haven't looked at them very carefully."

"Do they require care? That closet is not the Louvre."

"Isn't this room a work of art, Mr. Klingsburg? In the way it evokes a year, I mean?"

"Art is a point in time, but art is not a year. And nothing here could fool me that my youth is alive again, that the winter winds are not blowing for Klingsburg the Muralist."

"Do those items on the mantelpiece mean anything to you?"

The old artist stood up and peered at them. "We ate many nuts when our world was young. But we never stayed at the Astor. The dramas that moved us did not play the Criterion. And when we rode, others drove us, and the sobriquet of the vehicle was transient as dust."

"Is there any connection between them?"

"Connections are made on canvas, not on mantelpieces."

"What happened to Sally Jordan, Mr. Klingsburg?"

"What happens to anyone and to everyone. But too soon. I must take my leave. I sleep little, but I must rest before first light. Or last light."

Klingsburg seemed tired of the game he was playing. His spookily rarified manner of speech must have been a strain to keep up, even if he'd been practicing it all his life. Rachel was desperate for more information, which she was sure he had.

"Did Sally Jordan and Wilbur DeMarco marry?" she asked, knowing the answer but hoping somehow to prime the pump for more information.

"An irrelevant question. Did they lie together, is more to the point, and they surely must have, though I was not witness to such a coupling. They went not to the altar—she went to the barricades. In the eyes of government and propriety, Sally was married. Talk to her husband. He lives here in town."

Klingsburg dropped the news with such calculated casualness, Rachel was sure the bombshell effect was intended. She looked at Gil, who shrugged, disclaiming knowledge.

"What's his name?"

"Charles Freeman." For once giving a direct answer, Klingsburg spoke the name with contempt.

"Did Wilbur ever . . . ?"

"I've spoken enough. Gossip is not art. Turn off your memory machine." He gestured to the recorder on the table by the fire. "It turns its wheels endlessly still but hears nothing."

With that dramatic pronouncement, Klingsburg the Muralist was out into the night. As he followed the artist out the door, Gil Franklin mouthed, "I'll call you when I get home."

And Rachel was grateful when the phone rang some twenty minutes later. The fire was doing its best, but the 1937 room seemed very cold.

"Wasn't that a performance?" Gil said. His voice sounded a bit hollow.

"What a strange man," Rachel said.

"What a pretentious bastard, you mean. It's all an act. He really is a great artist, but Vern Speigel's still right to call him a fraud. He disparages gossip, but he got it in, didn't he?"

"I can't complain. It's what I wanted. It gives me a line of investigation."

"I never met this Charles Freeman and I pride myself on knowing just about everybody up here. I think I can find him for you, though."

"Thanks, Gil. Thanks for all your help."

"Can you sleep in that house after listening to that spook? He even scared me some. He's weird enough in the daytime, but by the fireplace, with the light glowing off his staring eyeballs—he could get work as a horror-movie jockey."

"You're right about that, but I'm fine."

"You could spend the night over here, if—"

"Gil, what will it take to convince you I'm not a cringing violet? I'm fine here, the door is locked, and I'm not afraid of ghosts."

"Okay, okay, see you tomorrow."

As soon as they hung up, Rachel was dialing the phone. But not, she told herself, because she still needed the reassuring sound of another human voice.

"Hello, Stu? I have a little more research for you to do. See what you can find on an actress of the '30s named Sally Jordan."

"Pictures?"

"I think so. She was married to a man named Charles Freeman. See if you can find anything on him, too."

"Will do. How's the article coming?"

"Oh, it's fascinating. You'll be coming up Friday?"

"Sure. And you'll be coming down Sunday?"

"You know I have another week to go. At least."

"Well, if you decide you've had enough, just say the word."

"I'm staying for the duration."

"Even if you solve your murder?"

"I still have to finish my research on 1937, don't I? I don't want all these people to think I've just been using them."

"Heaven forbid."

"Stu, I have one other approach to take."

"What's that?"

"What happened to Wilbur DeMarco's 1938 book? He was working on one in 1937. I've talked to two people today who knew him who told me he was. And yet it was never published. One of the people suggested he was putting people he knew from his political activities into the book as characters, maybe even using some real situation that he had been in. If the book was written and yet never published— well, maybe there's something in the manuscript that would give us a clue to what happened in 1937 that had such an effect on Wilbur."

"And where's the manuscript? Is there a copy in his house somewhere?"

"I don't think so. I've poked my nose just about everywhere it would fit. There are practically no personal papers of any kind, at least not dating back that far." She sighed. "It's hopeless. If the manuscript isn't here, where would it be? It probably doesn't exist any more, or if it does, he probably hid it in some safe-deposit box somewhere and I'd never have a chance of finding it."

"Who was his publisher?"

"Irvine and Campbell."

"They're still in the business. Why don't you call them? I doubt anybody's still employed there who was there fifty years ago, but they might be able to put you on to somebody."

"That's a great suggestion, Stu."

"Quit buttering me up. You could have thought of that without me. Now, don't you want to hear the fruits of my investigation?"

"Into Wilbur's Duesenberg? Yes, of course."

Stu recounted his interview with Dwight Purvis.

"Then it wasn't a 1937 car?" Rachel said.

"Purvis says not, and I think he knows his stuff. Do you think it means anything?"

"It means Wilbur, who was so meticulous about acquiring only genuine 1937 artifacts made an exception with that car. And there's something else. Dorie Moss told me she had the feeling Wilbur didn't even like the car."

"It's a thing of beauty, Rachel. Hard not to like. I wish I could've driven it away from Purvis's place myself."

"Maybe Wilbur had a special reason for not liking it. Plus a special reason for wanting it for his collection. Stu, you'll have to investigate further."

"What do you suggest?"

"Go back to Arthur Blemker. Try to find out the history of that car *before* Wilbur had it."

Stu's sigh was long-suffering. "Made more work for myself, huh?" Rachel wasn't convinced. He was getting as caught up in this thing as she was.

10

SHORTLY AFTER SEVEN o'clock, a red-capped acorn wood-pecker provided his reliable machine-gun chorus on the outside of the house, and Rachel was an inadvertent early riser once again. Hoping to take advantage of the pre–eight A.M. long-distance rates, she was on the phone to Manhattan after one cup of coffee.

The third person she talked to in the offices of Irvine and Campbell was a secretary of long service to the firm and even longer memory.

"Wilbur DeMarco? I haven't heard that name in years."

"Can you tell me who edited his books?"

"Oh, certainly. It would have been Gus Warner for the first few—he was before my time—and then it was Hannah Spurgeon. She edited most of our mystery writers from about 1935 on."

"I don't suppose she's still with the firm . . ."

"Oh, yes," came the surprising answer. "She's been a part of Irvine and Campbell for fifty-three years. She started as a reader, just a kid, and was an editor in no time. She's sort of semiretired now, though, and only comes in to the office a couple times a week."

"Will she be there today?"

"Who knows? She's an institution and not held to a strict schedule. But she'd never come in before two in the afternoon."

"Can you tell me where I can reach her?"

"I can give you her home number. She wouldn't mind. But don't dare call her before noon. That's a firm rule."

"I promise. Thanks."

With no more to do for the moment on tracking down Wilbur DeMarco's last manuscript, Rachel had another cup of coffee and leafed through a 1937 issue of *American* that featured articles on the Dust Bowl, the young Olivia de Haviland, and whether employers preferred high-school or college graduates—there was no unanimity on the question. Then she prepared for her walk into town.

Rachel was glad to get away from the house for a while. The past wasn't luring her so much as it was making her claustrophobic, and she knew that what she was looking for was really in 1987, even if it had its roots in 1937.

It was about a half-hour walk to the center of Idyllwild. The spring air was crisp but not cold, and the wildlife were active—squirrels and lizards and scrubjays as well as the omnipresent woodpeckers. Jack Hooper jogged past her with a wave. "See you tomorrow," he said. She smiled and waved back.

Approaching downtown Idyllwild, Rachel came to a shopping area known as Strawberry Creek Square. There were businesses of diverse size on either side of the parking lot—a restaurant, a dealer in electronic gear and satellite dishes, a drugstore, a shoe shop, a video rental outlet—and the post office that was a central meeting place for the people of Idyllwild on weekday mornings.

She was looking at a community bulletin board next to the post office when a voice behind her startled her with a hearty "Good morning!"

She turned around and looked at the handsome face of Roger Payne. He was dressed in jeans and a flannel shirt and had a stack of mail in his hand.

"Oh, good morning," she said.

"Sorry if I scared you. I guess I'm always sneaking up on you, huh?"

"I hope not."

"How's the 1937 research going?"

"It's fascinating. I had no idea it would be so involving."

"Who've you talked to so far?"

Seeing no harm in it, Rachel named her three visitors of the day before.

"Dorie and Vern are good people, but that Klingsburg, oh my God. My mom knew him back in her movie days. She could tell you some stories." He gestured with the fistful of letters. "Got her some fan mail today. Would you believe she still gets it? Don't know how they find her. I'll give it to her, and she'll make all kinds of nasty cracks about the idiots who write it, but she loves it really. May even stoop to answer some if conditions are just right. Loves to know she's remembered. She'll enjoy talking to you, too. You are going to come and see her, aren't you?"

"Oh, yes, I'm looking forward to it."

"I have to warn you she'll be a little difficult at first, but once you get used to each other, you'll get along fine."

"I'm sure we will."

"Look, I was just about to have a piece of apple pie and some coffee. I missed breakfast. Will you join me?"

"For the coffee anyway," Rachel said and followed him into the pastry shop and restaurant next to the post office.

Moments later, Roger gestured toward the window with a forkful of boysenberry pie. "You see all of Idyllwild go by this window at this time or morning. Not having home mail delivery does wonders for the sense of community."

"Have you always lived up here?"

"Pretty much. When my mom married my dad, she retired from pictures—that'd be right after World War II. They had a place in Palm Springs. That's where I was born, in '56. I came as quite a surprise, my mother being over forty at the time. I don't think my father wanted kids, so he took a powder, and we moved up here."

"Was your father in motion pictures, too?"

"I know practically nothing about my father, except that his name wasn't famous. And his name wasn't Payne, either.

I preferred to take my mother's name, when I had the choice."

Rachel was restraining herself from asking some overly personal questions about Roger's relationship with his mother. He seemed to read her mind.

"Don't worry, Rachel," he said with a laugh. "I'm no Norman Bates. I love my mom, and I'd like to take care of her, but I'm real normal deep down, and when the right girl comes along, well, she'll have to take care of herself. My mom will, I mean."

"And would you leave Idyllwild?"

"Oh, like a shot. For the right girl." He was looking her in the eye with meaningful intensity. Rachel decided to continue to pretend this was a casual conversation on both sides of the table.

"What do you do for a living, Roger?"

His smirk was slightly embarrassed but perhaps less so than it should have been. "Mom has quite a bit of money, and I take care of mom."

"And if you found this 'right girl' and moved off the hill, what would you do then?"

He shrugged. "I could learn the book business."

"There are more profitable lines than the book business, believe me."

"I think if a husband and wife can work together, it's great."

"And I think you're too inclined to rush things." She wanted to kick herself. There were encouraging implications in the remark she hadn't intended.

"You're probably right. I can go slower. Did anybody ever tell you your eyes are beautiful? Brilliant as gemstones and warm as kindling on the fire."

Oh, brother. Certainly Stu Wellman never came up with rhapsodies like that, but she didn't welcome them, even from one who could deliver them with just the right combination of sincerity and self-mockery and was a consensus hunk by any objective standard. A newcomer saved her from figuring out what to say next.

"Good morning, folks!" It was Jud Crompton, smiling his insincere huckster's smile. "What a beautiful couple you make. Eat your heart out, Charlie and Di."

Rachel forced a smile. Although Jud's remark allied him with Roger, the younger man didn't seem the least bit glad to see him.

"How are you, Jud?" he said without enthusiasm.

The realtor sat down. "Care if I join you?"

"I think you already have."

Jud turned to Rachel. "How about it? Want to hear my memories of 1937?"

"Do you have any?"

"Not a one, but I could show you some of my baby pictures. Bought any good books lately?"

"No, I'm on vacation."

"Not much book trade up here, but occasionally something nice turns up. Would you like the services of a mountain book scout?"

"Doesn't the real-estate business keep you busy enough?"

"I like to diversify. If I find anything good, I'll send it down to you with Gil Franklin. I don't often get down myself. I won't offer you any books with little dimples in the back cover." He turned to Roger. "There was this little dimple in a first edition I offered her, just like the dimple in your chin, and she wouldn't buy it 'cause she said it wasn't a first edition."

"It wasn't," said Rachel.

"I have to admire people who stick to their guns even when they're wrong, don't you, Roger?"

"I don't know. It depends."

"I need to see your mom again, Roger. Can I come by?"

"Nothing stopping you."

Rachel could tell the two men were having a conversation between the lines, but she wasn't sure about what.

Jud turned to Rachel again. "Do any hiking?"

"Oh, sometimes."

"Some great trails up here. Stop by the office and I'll give you a map. And some tips, too. It helps to know the ropes, even if these are pretty easy trails, not rock climbs."

"I wouldn't go on the trail alone, though," said Roger.

"Maybe we'll try one on Saturday, when Stu comes up to visit," she said pointedly.

"The Devil's Slide is kind of a tough hike if you haven't done much walking lately," said Jud. "But the Deer Springs trail up to Suicide Rock might suit you fine. You have to get a wilderness permit over at the ranger station before you go up. Come by the office and I'll give you some information. I know all these trails like the palm of my hand. Do one with Alice every weekend." He stood up. "Well, I'll leave you folks to your little chat." He sauntered out.

"I detected a little hostility between you two," Rachel said.

Roger shrugged. "He's a pest and a know-it-all, but hostility's going a little strong."

"What does he want to see your mother about?"

"He's after some land she owns."

"On Meditation Point by any chance?"

Roger looked surprised. "Not far from there. How'd you know about it?"

"Lucky guess."

"I sure don't want to see that area developed."

"Does your mother?"

"Not sure she cares. She hardly ever leaves the house. But she sure doesn't need any more money. I hope she won't sell to him. You want to come see her this morning?"

Rachel looked at her watch. "I don't think I'll have enough time. I have an afternoon appointment, and I left my cassette recorder back at the house."

Roger looked dubious. "I don't know if mom will want to be recorded."

"Anyway, when I do come to see her, I don't want to have

to rush things."

"I don't want to rush things either, Rachel. With you, I mean. But thirty was kind of a traumatic birthday for me." Rachel restrained herself from agreeing that for him, it should have been. "You wouldn't understand that, because you aren't there yet. When I was going to high school down in Hemet, I knew a lot of girls. Took the prettiest girl in class to the senior prom. When I look at you, I can't even remember what she looked like." His face brightened. "Why don't you come to dinner some evening? I'll cook us a gourmet meal, show off my domestic skills. And mom's sometimes mellower in the evening."

She shook her head. "No thanks, Roger. An afternoon will be better." She assured herself she would visit chez Payne only in broad daylight.

When she'd extricated herself from the attentive Roger, Rachel walked a couple of blocks to the Puttering and Pans shop, a largish and messily eclectic emporium with some very classy gift and craft merchandise alongside kitsch as self-consciously cute as the place's name. A blank-faced late-teenage girl was sullenly attending the cash register, and she left her one customer alone.

All that changed when Alice Zimmer came sailing out of the back room. In everyday clothes and very light makeup, she looked paradoxically younger than when dolled up for the Town Prom.

"Well, hi!" she said cheerily. "How's that toe?"

"Healing up, thanks. This is quite a place you have here."

"We like to keep it warm and friendly," Alice said, casting a dubious glance at her zombielike employee. "Were you looking for anything special?"

"No, just looking."

"Well, come on in back and have a cup of tea." She led the way to a combination office-kitchenette, clearing a stack of invoices so Rachel could sit down. A kettle was blowing its first gust of steam on the stovetop, and a cutesy flowered teapot like several in the store's stock sat atop a trivet on the desk. Alice, apparently one who scorned the use of teabags, spooned some loose tea into the pot. "Lapsang Suchong," she said. "Hope you like it. It's my favorite."

"It'll be fine."

"Jud said he saw you over at the pastry shop." News certainly traveled fast in a small town. "He's real interested in your business. He collects first editions, did you know that?"

"Yes, he told me."

"He's always taking trips down to Hemet or Riverside looking for first editions. I didn't know they had so many bookshops there, did you?"

"There are a few," Rachel said noncommittally. If Jud was trying to keep some of his *sub rosa* development schemes from Alice, maybe the books were a handy excuse.

Alice was looking coy. "Jud's told me you and he had some little disagreement over a book. Men always have to be right, don't they? Sometimes I think they never grow up. I always think it's just as well to agree with them, unless it's something really important, don't you?"

"I'm not sure. But in this case, there were dollars and cents involved."

Alice laughed. "And that's really important. Oh, I know. I'm in business, too. Jud's so full of bluster, but he's a good man at heart. I don't think he'd really do anything wrong to anybody on purpose."

Why this line of discussion? Rachel wondered. What did Alice expect her to say? Maybe she just wanted Rachel to improve her opinion of Jud. But why would she care?

To change the subject, Rachel asked, "Have you lived in Idyllwild long?"

"Ten years. I think it's my natural environment. I'm a squirrel at heart. You can probably tell that by the store, huh?"

"Do you get down to the flatland much?"

"No more than I can help. My mother's one of those

people you read about on the society pages, doing good works and throwing charity balls and so forth. You've probably seen her. Mrs. Edgar Wilmington?"

"Oh, certainly." Rachel usually gave the society pages a wide berth, but the name was familiar to her.

"Edgar's not my father. My father died in the war, right after I was born. He was quite a hero, I guess." The statement was casual, but the pride in her voice was unmistakable. "My mother got lucky again the second time around, and I was brought up among the rich kids. Didn't come naturally to me. Maybe I took after my father, even if I never knew him. Anyway, I still go down to my mother's society shindigs a couple times a year—it's nice for a change, and I'm really proud of all the good things she does. Jud went to one with me once." She laughed. "He hated it. Which was just as well, because mother couldn't stand him either. Even though it's not really my scene, I can fit into the upper crust when I have to, but not Jud." She sighed. "He's a great guy really. I've been around, and I've known lots of guys, but Jud . . . I can't put my finger on it. Of course, you saw what a great dancer he is, and that means a lot, but . . ." She broke off.

It suddenly occurred to Rachel that this vivacious woman must be starved for someone of her own sex to talk to.

After an uncomfortable silence, Alice said, "There are people who'd like to poison my mind about Jud. I don't know why. They want me to believe Jud would turn our beautiful hill into a parking lot."

"You mean the rumors about developing Meditation Point?"

"Oh, I don't mean that. Of course, I don't agree with it, but it is private land, and if the owners want to develop it, I guess that's their business, and if some realtor is going to benefit by it, I guess it might as well be Jud. I wouldn't mind having a place with a view like that, would you? That's just business, like your books and my pans. And just because I'm a conservationist doesn't mean I'm some kind of a left-

92

winger who wants to stifle free enterprise. No, what people have tried to tell me is that he'd do things that were actually dishonest, circumventing building and zoning codes, bribing public officials, things like that. And I just can't believe that of a man like Jud, can you?"

"I don't know him very well," Rachel said carefully.

"I do. And I just can't believe . . ." She smiled again. "Jud can't keep anything from me. He tries, but he can't. He's tried to surprise me with presents, but I always get out of him what they are before Christmas or my birthday or whatever the occasion is. And when Jud makes a good deal, he just has to tell me about it, right away. He's so proud of himself when he pulls something off. He told me how he sold that book you wouldn't take for thirty or forty bucks. So proud of himself. But that's the way he is, like a little boy. I wouldn't want you to think badly of him."

"Of course not," Rachel said.

"I love it up here—every squirrel and every tree and every little waterfall. I don't want it to change. And I know Jud feels the same way. He couldn't fool me about that."

Rachel didn't answer. She had no reassurance to offer.

11

WHEN RACHEL HAD walked back to the house, it was around one o'clock, just time to have a quick lunch and try the number of Wilbur DeMarco's old editor before her afternoon appointment arrived. She wouldn't be getting the long-distance off-hours break, but she was so anxious to talk to Hannah Spurgeon, she didn't care.

A pleasant and surprisingly young-sounding voice answered on the first ring.

"Is this Hannah Spurgeon?"

"Yes, it is."

"Ms. Spurgeon, my name is Rachel Hennings, and I was referred to you by Irvine and Campbell."

"About Wilbur DeMarco. Yes, they warned me. Actually, I've been waiting for your call. I haven't heard from Wilbur in years, but I have an address for him out there in California. If you do manage to talk to him . . ."

Rachel suddenly realized that she hadn't mentioned in her earlier call that Wilbur DeMarco had died. She found herself in the position of breaking the bad news, which she did gently, not knowing how close the woman had been to Wilbur. There was silence on the other end for a moment, and Hannah Spurgeon spoke in a voice thickened by emotion.

"Isn't it funny? We hadn't spoken or even sent Christmas cards in so long, but I feel such a loss knowing Wilbur's not around any more. You say he was murdered?"

"Yes."

"But who . . . ?"

"The police think an addict looking for drugs."

"That's the kind of thing that happens here in New York. But in a little town in the mountains, where he lived . . . ? Why wasn't it in the papers?" she said, almost angrily. "It should have been in the *Times*. He may be forgotten now, but Wilbur DeMarco was one of the best American mystery writers, even if he has been out of print for forty years. What did you say was your interest in Wilbur, Ms. Hennings? I think I must have missed that."

Rachel said nothing of her suspicions about DeMarco's death but described the article she was writing.

Hannah Spurgeon didn't sound charmed by the idea. "Living in the past. Not healthy at all."

"Perhaps not if taken in excess, but it can be therapeutic sometimes."

The woman's voice turned hard and businesslike as if by force of will. "I live for my next project. For fifty years, I've continued to think Wilbur DeMarco might be my next project once again. That he might return to writing. It was always an empty hope, and now that he's gone, I needn't indulge it any more." Her voice softened slightly. "Thank you for bringing me the news, Ms. Hennings. Was there anything else I can do for you?"

Not pointing out the woman had done nothing for her yet, Rachel said, "I understand Mr. DeMarco was working on another Henry Friday novel in 1937, for publication the next year. But it was never published."

"Of course it wasn't. It was never finished. You can't publish an unfinished detective novel, can you? No matter how good it is. Unless it's by Charles Dickens."

Rachel was almost holding her breath. "But you read the unfinished novel?"

"Yes, he sent me about half of it late in 1937. It was marvelous, and I told him so. It had a depth of character development to it, comparable to what Sayers and Allingham and the English were doing, something like what the Ellery Queen team were striving for then but poor old Van Dine

96

never even attempted. It was far better than Wilbur's earlier books, fun though they were. I couldn't wait to read the rest of it. Then he told me early in 1938, when his deadline had come and passed, that the book would never be finished, that he was done writing detective novels. Done writing anything at all, as it turned out."

"Did he tell you why?"

"No, not really," she said impatiently. "Something happened. He didn't really specify what it was."

"What did he say about it exactly?"

"You expect me to remember a conversation I had half a century ago, young woman?"

Rachel took a chance. "Based on what you've said so far, Ms. Spurgeon, I'm afraid I do. I don't think you'd forget anything that important about an author you'd helped, one whose work meant something to you."

The noise at the other end of the line could have been a snort or a chuckle, but it sounded appreciative. "You must be a good judge of people. All right, I do remember. Almost like it was yesterday. He said now that he'd encountered a real-life tragedy, now that he knew how it really felt, he never wanted to write about fictional crime again."

"Did he say what that crime was?"

"No, he obviously didn't want to, and somehow I didn't want to press him on the point. It was his work that mattered to me. I said, 'You must keep writing, Wilbur. You can write about crime better and more deeply than ever before if you can draw on your own experience.' I was probably sounding desperate and overdoing it and he thought that was funny. He said, 'Hannah, you forget, my readers are expecting Cortland Fitzsimmons, not Francis Iles.' You've never heard of those people of course—they were '30s mystery writers."

"I know," said Rachel. "I'm in the book business."

"Well, if you remember Cortland Fitzsimmons, you're in it up to your eyebrows. I told him he was miles better than Cortland Fitzsimmons and *could* be better than Francis Iles, but he said not if he didn't want to do it. That I couldn't argue with, I'm afraid. He never told me exactly what had happened, and I didn't press him. What did it matter? Either he kept writing or he didn't, and he didn't. When it became clear to everybody at I. and C. that the new book was never coming, after Wilbur had returned his advance—that's the kind of man he was, how many writers ever return an advance? When that happened, I remember somebody in the office saying it was the old story of the writer ruined by Hollywood. But he quit screenwriting, too, and anyway, he wrote that first half while he was in Hollywood and it was the best thing he'd ever done, so I could hardly agree with the stereotype, could I?"

"Does that manuscript still exist, Ms. Spurgeon?"

"It certainly does. Let me assure you I'm not the sort of person who keeps all manner of things for their sentimental value, but an excellent piece of writing is another matter."

"Could you possibly send me a copy of the manuscript?"

"Of course I could, if you want to read it. How soon do you need it?"

"As soon as possible."

"Suppose I send it express mail? You'll have it by Thursday."

"That would be wonderful. But maybe you'd better send it to Stu Wellman." She gave his address at the *News-Canvass*.

"A newspaper reporter." Rachel could almost hear the wheels turning in the editor's head. "So there's some publicity in the offing?"

"No. I just think that would be the most convenient way to get it to me. He's driving up on Friday, and I'm not sure how the mail works up here in Idyllwild."

"Can you *get* it some publicity? It can't hurt Wilbur now, and maybe it could help him to get back into print. That's something I've wanted to see for years, but Wilbur didn't seem to want his books reprinted. Perhaps we can even pub-

98

lish the unfinished book. Have someone write an ending for
it, maybe, though I can't imagine who could do the job."

"I'm really looking forward to reading that manuscript,"
Rachel said.

"For its literary qualities? I'm helping you, young woman,
but you aren't being completely candid with me. What's really going on here?"

"To put it simply, I don't think a young addict killed Wilbur DeMarco, and I think the motive for his murder might
be in that manuscript."

Hannah Spurgeon was unimpressed yet again. "What
nonsense. But I'll send it, and if you do find out anything, be
sure to keep me posted, won't you?"

"Of course. Thanks so much."

"Just do right by Wilbur. He was a wonderful man,
wonderful writer. I'll get the manuscript out to you tomorrow."

Rachel hung up the phone, excitement rising. How could
she stand the wait until Stu brought that manuscript Friday
night? Fortunately there was plenty to do. Gil Franklin was
pulling into the driveway with her next interview subject.

12

RACHEL DROPPED INTO a chair in the 1937 room, breathing hard. She gestured helplessly toward the cassette recorder on the coffee table. "Can't start yet," she gasped. "Got to get my breath first."

Ernest Basset shook his head. "My, my. You gotta get yourself in shape, Rachel, little dance like that tire you out."

"It must be this altitude."

"Oh, yeah, sure it is." Basset had just given her the lesson in the Big Apple that had been postponed at the Town Prom in the interest of public safety. The old dancer was still remarkably limber. "I'm a creaking old fossil compared to what I was, but it gives you an idea of the big '37 dance. It was a real short-lived craze, sort of like the twist. Old hat by the end of the year. Guys that really liked to show off on the dance floor were called 'shiners'—I don't think that was either a reference to black eyes or to people of color, but then again, maybe it was."

After a moment, Rachel managed to catch her breath enough to switch on the recorder and do her standard introduction. "Mr. Basset, what do you remember . . . ?"

"Stick to Ernest. Not Ernie, though."

"Ernest, what do you remember about 1937?"

"You kids think that was the Stone Age, don't you. Well, let me tell you—we had refrigerators then and a few color movies and the Hudson people were advertising a car with an automatic transmission, though I can't say I ever drove one. Why, most of us had actual indoor plumbing, even us black folks. Over in England, they already had television. We didn't have computers or moon rockets, 'cept in the pulp magazines and comic strips, but all in all it was *almost* modern times."

"You were working in motion pictures in 1937?"

"I got what work I could there, and I can tell you it sure beat vaudeville. Not to mention floor sweeping, cotton picking, and shoe shining. That year I got a nice job at MGM, I remember, on a picture called *A Day at the Races* with the Marx Brothers. I was one of the dancers in the 'All God's Children Got Rhythm' number. They always cut that number when they show it on TV. It's supposed to be racist, you see, and I guess it is." He said it grudgingly. "The black stereotype in its purest form. It's got us gamblin', rollin' our eyes, singin' spirituals, jitterbuggin', and celebratin' our natural sense of rhythm like all get out. But I still wish they wouldn't cut it any more. The talent up there on the screen in that number was awesome, some of the best black singers and dancers around at that time, and that little segment of film, Rachel—well, it's our immortality. People shouldn't deny us that. In that little piece of film, I'm as limber and agile as I ever was and I can do things with my body that hardly anybody can do and look graceful doin' it. I'm only in the spotlight for about twenty seconds, but I surely do use the time. People ought to be able to look past the stereotypes and see the talent that was there.

"At least we were really black. Amos 'n' Andy were at their peak then on the radio. They used to say on a hot summer evening between seven and seven-fifteen, you could walk down the street and not miss a second of the show, coming out of people's open windows. Can't say I ever tried it."

"Was that true in black neighborhoods, too?"

"Good question. Some black people listened, I know that, and some of 'em even liked it. Proud of whatever little crumb of the 'black experience' managed to get on national radio. I could get a laugh out of it myself once in a while, in a weak moment. By '39, at least those two black-talkin' white guys were giving some genuine black actors work on the show."

"Did you ever meet Wilbur DeMarco back then, Ernest?"

"No, we traveled in different circles you might say. Black folks in show business could make plenty of money in those days—at least, a select lucky few could. But however much moolah we might have raked in, however much fancy stuff we could buy with it, we were living in a separate world. Oh, I know they say Wilbur was a great liberal and all that, and I know there was some Hollywood money helping to fight against lynching and Jim Crow in the South, so I'll give him his due. But I don't think there were very many black faces at those tony parlor-radical parties he went to. It was sort of like what they called 'radical chic' in the sixties, I think."

"You didn't like Wilbur?"

"I liked Wilbur a lot. Up here, I mean. But back then, I don't know if I would have or not."

"How did you know about the parties he went to?"

"Hollywood was almost like a plantation in those days, Rachel. And us out in the servants' quarters knew all kinds of things about what the folks in the big house were up to."

"Do you know who else went to those parties?"

"What are you, Rachel, HUAC?"

She laughed. "HUAC?"

"House Un-American Activities Committee. You young people don't know your history."

"I know what HUAC was, and I'm not it. Just a neophyte magazine writer."

"What's neophyte mean? Nosy?"

Rachel knew he was having fun with her and didn't mind. "I think you know what it means, Ernest," she said in a mock-acerbic tone. "All I'm trying to do is get a picture of what Wilbur's world was like, since this project's dedicated to him."

"Well, he had a lot of good points," Ernest said, deadpan. "Maybe even back then."

"You said he was a jazz fan, didn't you?"

102

"Oh, my, yes. We used to talk about jazz and big-band music a lot since I knew him up here."

"Did you come here to talk about jazz with Wilbur?"

Ernest nodded his head. "Once or twice. Not often. He played me some of his old 78s once. It was something. Not just hearing the music, which was great, but seeing those old black discs goin' fast around the turntable. Any idea what's going to become of those records? I guess they're still here."

"I'll ask Wilbur's cousin, Arthur Blemker. Maybe he'd give you a chance to acquire them."

"Thanks. No offense to your little machine, Rachel, but tape cassettes just don't get it as far as I'm concerned."

"This one's got about all it can hold," she said, switching it off. "Ernest, what do you think really happened to Wilbur? Who do you think killed him?"

There was a pained expression on Basset's face. "I don't know, Rachel. You think it was a personal motive?"

"I don't know, either, but there are a lot of people up here who were around Hollywood in the '30s."

"Including me. But I don't think most of us knew Wilbur. Personally anyway. I know Jack Hooper didn't."

"What about Frances Payne?"

"Never met the lady but once. Can't say we hit it off too well. When you're a member of a minority, Rachel, you get like a sixth sense. You can always tell when the color of your skin makes a difference to people. It's not anything special they do or say, but you just know. Frances Payne's the kind of lady I got to either shake my fist at or give her a wide berth. In my present aged and mellow condition, I choose to give her a wide berth."

"Do you know William Klingsburg?"

"The painter? Oh, yeah. Crazy guy."

"He knew Wilbur in 1937."

"Another political type. I've met Klingsburg once or twice, but he didn't strike me as somebody you could have a conversation with."

Rachel felt the corners of her mouth twitching.

"You found that, too, I bet," Ernest said.

"Yes, I found that, too. Do you know a man named Charles Freeman?"

"Wasn't he either Amos or Andy on the radio? No, no, that was Freeman Gosden and Charles Correl."

"You're playing games with me again, Ernest."

"No such thing. Don't know the man. I'd say if I did. I think I know what you're trying to do, Rachel, and I guess I'm not much help."

"I'm just trying to capture a year, Ernest, and you've been a very big help. Did Wilbur have that display on the mantelpiece when you were here?"

Ernest stood up and walked over to look at the car, key, tickets, and peanut can. "I don't remember it."

"Does that combination of items mean anything to you?"

"Well, now, let's see. Show's over, this ain't no hotel, I gotta get in my car and drive away, 'cause it's time for you to eat. How's that?"

Rachel laughed. "Wrong. Show's just beginning. You can stay as long as you want, and anyway you didn't bring your car because Gil brought you. I want you to stay for dinner, and we're not just having peanuts."

Ernest grinned. "That reminds me. George Washington Carver was another cat who was real big in '37. But he and Booker T. Washington never could get along."

13

When Stu's call came at about nine o'clock that evening, Rachel could tell immediately he had plenty to tell her and was going to take his time about telling it. That was no problem. It would be nice to listen to him talk while she watched the fire flicker. He was paying for the call, and her interviews with the Idyllwild seniors were accustoming her to verbal cat and mouse. Let Stu take his time.

First, maddeningly restrained, he insisted on a description of her interviews to date, which she provided in detail. When she told him about Hannah Spurgeon and Wilbur's reference to real-life crime, Stu punctuated her account with knowing "hmmm" and "ah" noises. He clearly thought he had something.

"You'll be getting a copy of Wilbur's last manuscript in the mail," Rachel said. "When you get it up here Friday night, we can pore over it together."

"Suppose I jump the gun and read it first, since you're using me as an accommodation address," Stu said.

"Sure, go right ahead, but let me form my own conclusions."

"I'll give you something to form your own conclusions about, my dear."

"I'm glad I can't see the canary feathers on your chin. It must look disgusting. Did you find out some more about Wilbur's Duesenberg?"

"Inquiries are proceeding on that. Arthur Blemker got it from the estate of an art director who used to work in the studios. The art director's son was born in 1935, so his memo-

105

ries of '37 are sketchy, but he had the idea the car had belonged to Americana Pictures at one time and they'd let his dad have it for a song. Of course, there is no Americana Pictures any more, so I'm not sure where to go from there." He seemed to want to get the car question out of the way in a hurry.

"I take it the bombshell you're preparing to explode has nothing to do with the car. Are you good and ready to explode it now?"

"Certainly. Rachel," he said carefully, "you've got a lot of *Life* magazines up there, haven't you?"

"Yes. They're terrific. *Life* was new in 1937."

"All the issues you have are '37 ones, right?"

"Sure. What would Wilbur want with anything published any other year?"

"I have in front of me a copy of *Life* for the first week of 1938. What do you think was the last major event of 1937?"

"Well—"

"Come on, it's obvious. What's the last thing that happens any year?"

"New Year's Eve parties, I guess."

"Right. And the parties for New Year's Eve 1937 were the biggest and most enthusiastic and most expensive since 1928, the last New Year's before the stock market crashed. People were getting a feeling prosperity was returning, the Depression was winding down. They had plenty of clues that war in Europe was likely, of course, but they had the idea they could bring back boom times without Hitler's help."

"You sound like you're getting downright enthusiastic about the period, Stu. Get on with it. What have you found out? You have before you a copy of *Life* . . ."

"Yes. I have a wide-angle picture of Times Square in New York as the mobs were ringing in 1938. The shot is dominated by two companies who had huge advertisements there, looking down on the crowds."

Rachel had it in a flash. "Chevrolet and Planter's

Peanuts!" she exclaimed.

Stu sounded so deflated, Rachel was sorry she'd anticipated his announcement. "You knew it all the time," he said.

"I didn't, but I should have. Vernon Spiegel told me the Criterion Theatre and the Hotel Astor were near Times Square. So as soon as you said two advertisers—"

"Okay, okay. So you know that DeMarco's mantel display was all about Times Square. But do you know why?"

A note of impending revelation was creeping back into Stu's voice.

"No, of course I don't. Let's hear the rest of it."

"First of all my research assignments. Sally Jordan was an actress who came to Hollywood from Broadway in 1934. She was a beauty and the object of much attention from every eligible bachelor in town, if you believed the gossip columnists. But she was also a bit of a maverick, too outspoken for her own good, always complaining she wasn't getting good enough roles. In one interview, she was quoted as saying, 'I didn't learn classical acting just so I could make my living screaming.' She didn't make herself too popular with the studios, but she was liked by the public and she had a lot of friends in town. She seems to have been respected as a genuinely concerned person. By 1937, she was speaking out pretty regularly on social issues and got involved with liberal causes. She participated in benefits to support union organizing, to aid the Loyalists against Franco in Spain, all the usual stuff. That, I trust, is where she got to know Wilbur DeMarco and that is why you asked me to find out about her, am I right?"

"They might have been in love, Stu."

"Ah, but she was married, and she undoubtedly had a morals clause in her contract."

"What did you find out about Freeman?"

"Eldest son of a banking family, born 1910. By all accounts, their marriage in 1936 came as a big surprise to everybody, her friends, his family, the gossip columnists. Freeman enjoyed the company of beautiful young women, and they enjoyed the company of his money. But he was not a particularly handsome lad and about as hidebound and stodgy as a guy in his mid-twenties could be. Obviously, he was nuts about Sally. Had to be. But he must have been embarrassed by a lot of her activities."

"Yet they stayed married?"

"Yes, they did." Rachel could tell from something in Stu's voice he had another bombshell to drop. No use guessing, she decided. Let him have his fun. "Of course, divorce wasn't entered into quite as casually in those days as it is today, even in Hollywood." The bright statement had misdirection written all over it. "During 1937, there was a left-wing political action group in Hollywood called the Committee for Freedom and Justice. Later identified as a Communist front, but who knows? They mostly raised funds that were used to support the unions, both those that were trying to get a foothold in the movie industry and some in other occupational groups. Sally Jordan was a prominent member. Of course, full membership was never made public. Even then, when the left was downright trendy, there'd be a lot of people who preferred to stay in the closet as far as their involvement was concerned. I suppose among the other members were some of those Hollywood radicals that got in so much trouble a few years later. It's the kind of thing that might have appealed to our friend Wilbur DeMarco, though I can't say for sure if he was a member."

"I'm willing to bet he was," Rachel said.

"You're probably right. The Committee disbanded in early 1938, by the way, and there were vague rumors of scandal, misappropriation of funds. I tried to find out what it was all about, but none of the available sources could tell me the whole story. One thing I do know is that a writer named Monte Fanning committed suicide in March of '38—he'd been a member of the group, and rumor had it he was the guy responsible for whatever siphoning off of funds had gone on. But the full story was never made public.

"Anyway, in late '37, Sally Jordan was in the last stages of a long-term contract and getting more and more popular with the public, but when her contract ran out, instead of signing another one with the studio, she surprised everybody by taking a part in a Broadway play. It was called *Barricades*."

Rachel remembered Klingsburg's veiled reference to Sally "going to the barricades." Very cute. "What kind of a play was it, as if I didn't know?"

"Typical socially conscionable tirade of the times, I guess, Clifford Odets kind of thing. Must have been softened up a bit for Broadway, though. She was quoted as saying she felt she owed it to herself and the public to appear in a play that made an important statement about the times and the aspirations of the common people, et cetera, et cetera. At least she restrained herself from saying 'the masses.' Anyway, it opened late in the year. Got pretty good reviews and seemed settled in for a long run. Thus, Sally was in Manhattan that New Year's Eve." Stu paused dramatically, and Rachel could feel exasperation rising.

"Stu, will you get to the point? You're starting to remind me of Klingsburg the Muralist."

"What?"

"Never mind. Sally was in Manhattan that New Year's Eve."

"Yeah. I imagine a Broadway star would have had invitations to a lot of celebrations, but she was a woman who identified with the common people, and she went where the common people went. And that was Times Square, right in the middle of that crushing crowd under the Planter's Peanuts sign."

Rachel had a sudden feeling she didn't want to hear what came next, and she felt a slight irritation at Stu's customarily facetious matter. These were real people they were talking about after all.

"What happened, Stu?" she asked in a flat voice.

As if reading her thoughts, Stu sounded more serious. "She was murdered. Stabbed to death. Nobody ever found out who killed her. Rachel, that was Wilbur's real-life crime!"

That night Rachel hauled out Wilbur DeMarco's collection of posters to give them a closer look. They seemed to have taken on a new importance. And she wasn't surprised that one of them, among all the movie lobby posters, proclaimed a Broadway opening. Sally Jordan, forgotten now, had been big enough then to have above-the-title billing in *Barricades*, her leading man, Eric Chambers, relegated to smaller print below the title.

Several of the movie posters featured Sally Jordan, too. She had been a beauty all right, black-haired, lush-lipped, high-cheekboned, but something about her face, in photographs or in artist's renderings, invariably suggested intelligence and humor. Not hard to imagine she was someone the young Wilbur DeMarco could have been in love with.

Near the bottom of the stack of posters was one Rachel decided ought to go on display for her next interview subject.

14

JACK HOOPER HAD finished his morning run and was dressed for polite society when Gil Franklin dropped him off on Wednesday morning. His white jacket and peppermint-striped trousers suggested a band musician ready to play an old-fashioned summer concert in the park. A straw hat would have made a nice addition to his wardrobe.

"Why's Gil running this ferry service anyway?" Hooper asked, when they were seated in the living room. "I told him I could take my own car over here or just walk, but he kinda insisted his chauffeuring was part of the deal."

Rachel smiled. "He's my protector."

"And why would you need one of those?"

"I don't. Gil's just a gentleman of the old school. Let's get started. Up to now, I've just been asking my subjects for general memories of 1937, but in your case, I have something I want to show you, see what memories it brings back."

"Sure, okay." Jack Hooper seemed a bit wary.

Rachel switched on the recorder, telling it the date and the name of her subject. Then she pulled out the movie poster from under the coffee table. She'd expected to surprise Hooper with it, but was she only imagining that an expression of relief came over his face when he saw it?

For the benefit of the tape recorder, Rachel said, "I've now unveiled an old poster for a film called *Murder at the Snowline*, based on one of Wilbur DeMarco's Henry Friday novels. The poster illustration shows the distinguished movie and stage star Albert Melton in the role of Henry Friday, which he played in several films, but it also shows the romantic male lead, played by a handsome young actor named Jack Hooper, and the female lead, played by Estelle Graves. I'd think this was quite a collectors' item, wouldn't you, Mr. Hooper?"

"I'm not much of a collector," Jack Hooper said. "Nice poster, though, isn't it, with that creepy shadow falling over us, Estelle looking pretty and frightened? Come to think of it, I look plenty scared, too—the poster artist could make me a good actor, even if half the directors in Hollywood never could. The publicity people did a heck of a job with those things."

"What can you remember about making that film?"

"I don't remember much, I'll tell you that. I was in one quickie after another that year. It was assembly-line stuff on the B pictures in those days, sort of like TV series segments today. The pain those people went through trying to teach me how to act on the fly! Say, though, I do remember something about *Murder at the Snowline* at that." He laughed. "It was made right in the middle of summer, and the setting was supposed to be a snowed-in ski lodge in February. In those days, nobody went on location for much of anything. Everything was shot on the lot, even phony snowstorms. So there we were dying from the L.A. summer heat, dressed up in heavy sweaters and parkas trying to act cold. I tell you, they just demanded too much of my acting."

"Was Wilbur DeMarco ever on the set?"

"Not that I was aware of. I'm just about sure I never met Wilbur in those days, but to tell you the truth, if you'd asked me before you hauled out that poster, I'd have told you I never worked on a Henry Friday picture. So maybe I did meet him and just don't remember. They kept me so busy, I didn't know what I was doing."

"What did you do in your spare time?"

"Had fun. Went to the beach as much as I could. I didn't mix with the Hollywood people very much. They were just too phony for me. I wasn't interested in wild Hollywood par-

112

ties, and I sure didn't want to mix in politics, in or out of the studio." His face saddened for a moment. "That girl in that poster, Estelle. I was kinda in love with her in 1937. We went to the beach together a few times, and away from the sets and the lights, she was a heck of a sweet girl. Like a real person. But she was too much in love with 'the industry' and all that meant to let me take her away from it. And that was what you did with girls in those days, took 'em away from things. Not like now, huh?"

"No, not like now."

"I'm probably old-fashioned, but it might have been better if I had. She married a band leader after we broke up, then divorced him and married a press agent, then divorced him and married a guy that owned a couple of casinos in Vegas. Heck of a life, huh? She hung on in pictures as long as she could and killed herself in 1949. Pills. Officially an accident." He smiled painfully, trying to force his way back to his normal cheerfulness. "Life's kinda full of accidents, isn't it? It was only on the track I ever thought I could make things happen."

"Which reminds me that you were signed to a film contract after an amateur athletic career. I know in those days track-and-field athletes really did have to be amateurs. Was it good to have money in your pocket for a change?"

Hooper looked sheepish. "I'm afraid you're jumping to conclusions. I always had money in my pocket. My family was very well off. My father was a self-made multimillionaire—made a killing in real estate out here before World War I—and gave me all the money I wanted for just about whatever I wanted it for. He had plenty of money to throw around, and he probably contributed more to Republican candidates out here all through the '30s and '40s than any other individual. I didn't have to sign that picture contract in order to eat, I can tell you that."

"Did your family approve of your decision to get into the movies?"

"They kinda shrugged their shoulders and hoped I wouldn't embarrass them. The quality of performances I put on the screen embarrassed *me*, you understand, but that wasn't the kind of embarrassment they were worried about. They just didn't want me involved in any paternity suits, drunk-driving arrests, gambling raids, things like that."

"And what about politics?"

"Oh, they wouldn't have minded that if I stuck with the G.O.P. Fortunately, though, I was about as politically minded as Mickey Mouse." He smiled. "I'll tell you, Rachel, I was a kinda boring fellow. I think I was a nice enough guy, though. I had an old-fashioned morality. I was no sexual innocent, and I did my best to get Estelle into bed with me, but when she said no, no was it."

"What did you do for fun, besides the beach?"

"Estelle and I would go to the Pacific Coast League baseball games to see the old L.A. Angels and Hollywood Stars play and to the USC football games and out to Santa Anita to bet two dollars tops on the horses and listen to Joe Hernandez call the races. He was a better actor than I was."

"A lot of Hollywood people went to the races in those days."

"Oh, sure, and Estelle would spot every one of them and insist on saying hello. Table hopping. That was one reason I quit taking her out there. The other reason was I couldn't pick a winner to save my life—that's not the track I could make things happen on."

"When did you finish your movie career?"

"The studio heads finished it for me early in 1938. I was working for one of the majors, and I probably could have gotten some work on Poverty Row, Monogram or someplace like that, while my name still meant something, but what was the point? I didn't need the money. I followed my father into real estate and did pretty well—with him around, it would have been hard not to. I was all over the place during the war and managed to come out in one piece. I've been married twice, divorced twice. Never did find another Estelle. And I guess I was never really happy until I started running again, just a few years back. Some people I used to compete with think old-timers meets are ridiculous, but I enjoy them."

"That's what matters."

"If it's good enough for Senator Cranston, it's good enough for me. He's really a heck of a nice guy, even if my old man never would have voted for him. But hey, we're supposed to be talking about 1937, aren't we? I could tell you about Coast League baseball, if you want. It wasn't like going to see the Dodgers, but I think it was more fun."

"Sure, I'd love to hear about it," Rachel said and committed herself to a half hour of horsehide memories. At least her patient listening would allay his suspicions about any ulterior motives she might have in her questioning.

When it seemed natural, she brought things back to the Hollywood/Idyllwild connection. "Did you know any of the other local residents when you were working in films?"

"Gosh, I don't think so. Like who?"

"William Klingsburg, the painter."

"I've seen him around here, but I sure wasn't aware of him back then."

"What about Frances Payne?"

"Roger's mom? I just remember her from pictures. Heck of a good-looking gal, but we worked at different studios, and I only saw her on the screen, if at all."

"What about Sally Jordan?"

"Sally—does somebody by that name live up here?"

"No, but I thought you might remember her."

"I've never heard of her. Why should I have?"

"She was pretty well known."

"Not to me."

"And she was married to a man who lives up here. Charles Freeman?"

"Don't know him. Your friend Gil Franklin knows all the birds *and* all the people up here. I just know a few of each.

115

Sorry, Rachel, but I am one heck of a lousy witness to my times. However, I'm encyclopedic on the Pacific Coast League and college football. Want to hear about a few memorable USC games?"

She didn't, but she did.

15

I⊤ wasn'⊤ long after Jack Hooper had left with the Gil Franklin taxi service that Rachel's phone rang. The voice on the other end belonged to Arthur Blemker, Wilbur DeMarco's cousin.

"Hi," he said, "how's the sleuthing going?"

"I'm not sleuthing, Mr. Blemker. I'm . . ."

"Sure, sure, I know. Taking good care of my books, I hope. Not getting the pages dog-eared, are you?"

"No, but I'm reading them. They're meant to be read, right?"

"I find a baloney sandwich makes a nice bookmark."

"I'll be sure to try it."

"Listen, the reason I called is, I just got the goddamnedest call from New York. Woman at Irvine and Campbell, Wilbur's old publisher. They're talking about reprinting some of Wilbur's stuff in paperback and publishing Wilbur's unfinished last novel, getting permission from the estate to have somebody else finish it. What do you think of that?"

"I think it's a very nice idea."

"Oh, sure, so do I, but that's not what I mean. What put a bee in their bonnet about it now?"

"Well, Mr. Blemker, I did talk to someone there about your cousin's last novel. I'd heard from a couple of people who knew him that he was working on one, and I was just curious about what happened to it."

"Just curious. But you're not sleuthing, right?"

"Not exactly."

"And your friend from the *News-Canvass* who keeps

asking me questions about Wilbur's Duesenberg, he's not sleuthing either?"

"Just interested in old cars, I guess."

"Interested on your instructions. I gave him all the information I could, I want you to know. I'm intrigued by the whole business myself. It just seemed sort of funny. First Wilbur dies, supposedly done in by some kid junkie, then all of a sudden there's your magazine article, and then his old flame comes out of the woodwork . . ."

"His old flame? What do you mean?"

"Hannah Spurgeon, his editor at Irvine and Campbell. Didn't I tell you about her? I never met her, but he told me about her once, only time he ever talked to me about one of his lady friends. Cute as a button, he said, four-foot-ten and ninety pounds and able to dominate a room full of high-powered publishing tycoons just by the force of her personality. I wished I could meet her back then, but now I'm not so sure. She was absolutely nuts about Wilbur, wanted to get in his shorts like she never wanted anything. He thought she was cute, like I said, but he had no romantic interest in her at all. Now all of a sudden, she calls me on the phone and wants to finish Wilbur and reprint Wilbur in paperback. It's like the past all coming back in one big wave."

"I thought you said you didn't know your cousin very well."

"I didn't. He never would have talked to me about any woman *he* was interested in. He could have been dating Greta Garbo when he was in Hollywood, and I never would have known anything about it. But he did tell me about this one who was such a pest to him, and he sometimes had to jolly her along because she was his editor and important to him professionally."

"Well, Hannah Spurgeon is the person I talked to, and she did seem somewhat upset at Wilbur's death, but I had no idea he was any more to her than a writer she'd edited and admired."

"You wouldn't have known from what she said to me,

118

either. Except I *did* know. Don't get me wrong. I'm real pleased at the idea of Wilbur's books getting back into print, and I'd like to read another Henry Friday story, even if somebody else does finish it. But I just thought this information might help you with your sleuthing, that's all."

"I'm not sleuthing, Mr. Blemker."

"No, no, I'm sure you're not. But remember, that dollar rent is on the condition you let me know when you solve it. Right?"

"You've been very kind. I'll send you copy of my article."

"Just don't leave out the last chapter. Bye, Rachel."

She hung up the phone and pondered. Hannah Spurgeon had claimed to have no idea what crime had changed Wilbur DeMarco's life. Her ignorance hadn't seemed so unlikely as she explained it, but maybe she did know what happened and had a reason not to say. Maybe she had a motive to make it happen. Maybe she had been in Times Square on New Year's Eve of 1937. Maybe . . .

The doorbell rang. Rachel was surprised, because Gil hadn't made an afternoon appointment for her. She walked to the door and opened it to find Roger Payne standing there grinning at her.

"Hi, Rachel."

"Hello, Roger. Uh, how are you?"

"Just fine. I was just passing by, and I thought if you didn't have any plans for this afternoon you might like to come over and visit mom. I know it's short notice to make arrangements, but, well, she has her good days and her bad days, and I think today is kind of a good one. How about it?"

Rachel knew Gil Franklin would think she was crazy for going to an interview without leaving the customary trail of popcorn, but she didn't really feel endangered by Roger Payne and his mother, at least not by any danger she couldn't handle. And her curiosity about the mysterious Frances Payne was getting stronger and stronger. So after a moment's thought, she agreed. "Sure, why not? Look, should I bring

119

the recorder or not?"

"Oh, you can bring it. Mom may surprise us both and want to set it all down on tape for the ages. She's got some stories to tell, I'll tell you that." Roger glanced around the room. "Hey, this is really something, isn't it? And I thought *mom's* taste in decoration was old-fashioned."

"Did she ever visit here?"

"Not likely. I don't think I could name a private home in Idyllwild she *has* visited, though she'd go to a town event once in a while. Not in the last two or three years, though." He looked worried. "Sometimes I wonder what'll happen to her if I ever have to leave her. She could take care of herself, and she's sure not crazy or senile or anything, but she seems to get more and more reclusive. To tell you the truth, Rachel, I think your visit will be good for her."

"I hope so. Well, shall we go?"

Roger paused for a second. She had the feeling he was hoping to stay in the DeMarco house a little longer, maybe while she changed her clothes. But the jeans and blouse she had on were just fine for visiting an old movie star or any other purpose, and she didn't want to press her luck about Roger's libido.

The mode of transportation was a canary yellow pickup truck like many Rachel had seen on the mountain roads. It was as polished and cared-for as if it had been a classic Rolls-Royce. Even the bed of the truck glittered, and she had the feeling Roger would be far too meticulous ever to let a dog ride in it.

Roger let her in the passenger side in courtly fashion before coming around to take his place in the driver's seat. Before starting the engine, he grinned across at her, white teeth gleaming, and said, "That dinner invitation is still open for after your interview."

"Oh, thank you, but I won't be able to stay tonight."

"Well, if you change your mind, it'll stay open." He started the truck, made a quick U-turn, and shot along the road.

120

Roger drove too fast, as Rachel thought many of the locals did on the narrow, winding, mountain roads. By the time he pulled up in front of his mother's tree-shaded home, he had made several bewildering turns, and Rachel hoped she didn't wind up in the position of having to find her way home.

The Payne house was only one story, but it appeared to cover a great deal of square footage, and judging by the generous expanse of trees front, back, and sides, it probably came with several acres of land. Unlike Wilbur DeMarco's house, it had no view of anything but the surrounding trees, and it seemed doubtful much sun ever got to it.

Roger escorted her up the path to the front door. He opened it with his key, swung the door open, and gently called, "Mom, we have company."

Not waiting for an answer, he ushered Rachel inside, sitting her down in a dark and rather oppressive sitting room—the old-fashioned term seemed to fit. There was one shaded window. In direct contrast to much modern furniture, the four old upholstered chairs looked comfortable and weren't.

"Mom will be in in a minute," Roger said softly. "Make yourself at home."

Rachel didn't know whether the irony she heard in his voice was imagined, but it struck her as a perfect caption for a Charles Addams cartoon. She looked around the room. There was one bookcase, full of what could either be old 78 r.p.m. record albums or scrapbooks. On one wall was a portrait of the young Frances Payne, either by Vargas or someone with a very similar style. The room had more ashtrays than she had ever seen in one place, and though everything was spotlessly clean, it seemed to carry with it a permanent mustiness.

The wait for Frances Payne to appear was probably not as long as it seemed. In a way, warm though it was, it reminded Rachel of sitting undressed on a doctor's cold examination table for forty-five minutes. She wished the nurse (Roger) had let her stay in the waiting room (truck) until the doctor was actually ready to examine her.

What a foolish analogy, she told herself. I shouldn't be imagining myself naked with X ray-eyed Roger creeping around the place. She occupied herself for a moment by testing her cassette recorder, running on batteries today in case there was no electrical outlet handy. It worked fine, without the sepulchral echo the room seemed to call for.

At last, Roger and his mother came through the door. Frances Payne was a very large woman in a voluminous housecoat, and there was little in her puffy face to suggest the beauty on the wall.

"Mom, I want you to meet Rachel Hennings, the girl I told you so much about." Rachel found the statement distinctly odd. Wouldn't he have told his mother before they entered the room whom she was going to meet? Maybe the stilted tag was for Rachel's benefit.

"Hello, Miss Hennings," the former actress said. She spoke in a monotone, and her face had the same blankness about it. She sat down in one of the chairs and stared into Rachel's face for moment. "Pretty," she said, sourly and almost accusingly.

"Oh, yes," said Roger.

Frances Payne looked up at her son. "I'm not going to talk to her with you in the room. Go make yourself useful."

"May I bring you some tea, Rachel?"

"I can take care of all the amenities, Roger," his mother said. "I know you have work to do."

"Of course. I'll see you later, Rachel." He disappeared, not seeming visibly bothered by what Rachel saw as his mother's rudeness.

When Roger was gone, no tea was offered. Frances Payne said, "Do you mind if I smoke?"

Rachel hated cigarette smoke and was glad most smokers these days were courteous enough not to inflict their habit on others. But the courtesy seemed an empty gesture in this case, and she wasn't about to tell this woman she couldn't smoke in her own house. "Not at all," she said.

Frances Payne lit up an unfiltered Camel. "So you want to take my Roger away from me," she said.

"What?" Rachel was astonished. "I certainly do not."

"You can have him if you want him. I can't stand him hanging around all the time. He's been more trouble than he's worth since the day he was born. It was a damned difficult birth, let me tell you, and I was too old for motherhood anyway. When he was born, I no longer had my career, but I still had my figure. I don't think a body can bounce back from childbirth after forty as it can when it's younger. If it could I wouldn't be alone today. Or cooped up with Roger, which is worse than alone. Do you have children?"

"No, I'm not married."

"That's no answer these days. You've probably had a couple of abortions then."

"No, I haven't." Rachel sensed that letting this outrageous woman anger her would be playing into her hands, and anyway, the trend of the conversation was too interesting to make her angry.

"What do you use? Pill? IUD? Can't depend on the wretched devils to provide condoms, can you? It's the only way to go nowadays, with AIDS and everything. I'm almost happy to say I don't have to worry about that."

Rather than comment on her birth control methods, Rachel said, "Didn't Roger tell you what I wanted to talk to you about? I'm doing an article—"

"Article, huh? That's a new one. Let me tell you something for your own good, though you should be smart enough to figure it out for yourself. Doesn't it strike you that any thirty-year-old man who looks like Roger and is still living at home with his mother just has to be a loser? But, as I've said, you can have him if you want him. I'll be glad to be rid of him."

"Ms. Payne, I have no designs on your son, believe me. I just wanted to see you to . . ."

"What's this 'Miz' business? You from the South or something?" She waved her hand. "Oh, I know, I know, don't tell me. Call me Miss Payne or maybe Fran, if you're more comfortable with that, but when anybody calls me 'Miz,' all it does is remind me I missed getting the part of Scarlett O'Hara. By a whisker. If they hadn't brought in that English girl, I'd have had it, but a lot of good that does me now."

"Miss Payne, do you mind if I record our conversation?" She gestured to the cassette recorder.

"Well, let's talk about that. You actually are doing some kind of research here? That wasn't just a ruse to get close to Roger?"

"Yes, I am."

"Good. Then you must be smarter than you look. You have a good contract, I hope."

"A contract? Oh, you mean a publishing contract? No, I'm doing it on speculation. It may turn out to be just a labor of love."

"Labor of love! God, I love that phrase. You've already said you don't know anything about labor, and I doubt you know anything about love either. What are you going to do with the damned thing if you don't have a publisher?"

"I may have it privately printed, mostly for the people up here in Idyllwild who knew Wilbur DeMarco. It's a kind of memorial."

"Can't be much money in that. You can't be paying your subjects very much."

"Miss Payne, I'm afraid I'm not offering payment at all. I had no idea . . ."

"My God! So it's a labor of love for the victims, too, huh? Have you no understanding of the demands on a person's time? But I shouldn't be surprised. When I first came up here, I was anxious to be a part of the community, lend my presence to things, help in the best way I could. Then I went to one of their spaghetti feeds and found they expected me to *pay* for my spaghetti. Can you imagine that? Roger said,

124

let's just pay, we can afford it, but there was a principle involved. Don't they understand that when people in the public eye give of their *time*, it's as great a contribution as anyone else giving of their *money*? I said that day no more spaghetti feeds, no more pancake breakfasts, no more Town Proms. No more putting myself on exhibit for the yokels to stare at."

She lit another Camel with the glowing butt of the first. Apparently she only stopped smoking to move from room to room. "You are quite attractive, as Roger said."

"Uh, thank you."

"How old are you? Twenty-five?"

"That's about right."

"You won't always look like that, you know. Oh, you may not become a blimp like me, but the best you can hope for is the same general outline from fifty yards. You're going to puff out or shrivel up or maybe a little of both. That firm young body can't last you a lifetime. Those proud young breasts won't always stand up like sentinels, but how can I say that to someone of twenty-five? Nothing is more arrogant than youth!"

"Miss Payne, can I ask you a few questions about 1937? You see, Mr. DeMarco was very interested in that year . . ."

"It was an interesting year. But I don't know why I should give you a chunk of my memoirs for nothing when I could sell them tomorrow to any publisher in New York for six figures. Tell me why you think I should do that."

Rachel made herself smile. "I'm only asking for one year."

"But such a year." For the first time, there was a slight warmth in the actress's voice, a softening. "All right, I'll talk to you. I don't know why I should, but I will."

"Thank you. I do appreciate it." Rachel switched on her recorder and made the standard introduction. "Miss Payne, what do you most remember about 1937?"

"I was always traveling that year. The studio loaned me out to work on a picture in England. The British were doing some good work in those days, Hitchcock best of all, of course. The funding fell through, and the film never got made, but it was an exciting time to be in Britain, the time of the coronation of George VI. As an American film star, I was welcome everywhere and asked my opinion about everything, and I really admired the tradition of royalty, wished we had something of the kind here. So I was very popular with Fleet Street. They asked my impressions of Mrs. Simpson, and I gave them quite readily."

"Had you met her?"

"Not actually met her face-to-face, no. But I knew enough from people who did know her that I was terribly embarrassed by the black eye she was giving the United States of America with our staunchest allies, and I said so in no uncertain terms. I was good copy. God knows I tried to be. I'd comment on anything. There was just one thing I'd never give my true feelings about."

"What was that?"

"The wretchedly bad films I was appearing in and the lot of jackasses I had to work with to make them."

"Oh."

"God, how I hated Hollywood and everybody in it. If they weren't queers, they were reds. Sometimes they were both, the men, the women, all of them. Turn off that machine for a minute."

Rachel did so unquestioningly.

"Let me tell you something about Roger. He's totally worthless, but there's not a queer bone in him. I wouldn't tolerate his presence here if there were. I just wanted you to know that. He's still bad news, and I'm not recommending you respond to his advances—oh, what's the point? You've probably got your hooks in him already. But you're not getting my money, I'll tell you that. When Roger leaves here, and I wish he would, he makes his own way, and he can't do a damned thing. Just wanted to set the record straight on that. Turn it back on."

Rachel turned it back on.

126

"London was wonderful, and it didn't matter to me if I had work to do or not. The studio was paying my salary regardless. But transportation was a problem."

"In London?"

The mild question drew a withering glare. "No, not in London, you silly twit. There were plenty of cabs, and even the underground was rather fun. I meant transportation across the Atlantic. I had a terrible crossing going over, seasick every bit of the voyage. When the studio was ready for me to go back, I said I'd be damned if I'd face that again. I had to get my strength up, I said, before I'd do another Atlantic crossing and heave out my insides. That made them mad, of course—they said I was being difficult. Compared to some of the human flotsam stinking up the screen, I was a girl scout for cooperation, but this time I stood my ground."

"Was there plane service across the Atlantic yet at that time?"

"I don't know, but I wouldn't have considered it if there was. You could *not* get me up in an airplane."

"Didn't you like heights?"

"It wasn't the heights. The things weren't safe. They were always crashing, all through the '30s. Hardly a week went by you didn't hear of some mail plane or passenger plane going down somewhere or other. During the time I was in Britain, a seventy-one-year-old woman flyer disappeared—she had some kind of noble title. I don't remember what. And you know what happened to Amelia Earhart later that same year—well, we *don't* know what happened to Amelia Earhart, but you see what I mean. No, you couldn't get me in any airplane."

"What did the studio say when you refused to sail home?"

"What could they say? I had clout. I was first in line for Scarlett O'Hara, whatever anybody tells you. And Selznick would have had to pay Americana a bundle for my contract. They came up with a compromise. They said they could bring me home on the train. I said, since when is there a train that crosses the Atlantic? And they said, well, it's just like a train. Or like a ship without the rolling and turbulence. I'd sleep in a cabin that was just like a Pullman compartment, eat great food, watch the scenery go by, be back in New York in about three days. As they described it, it sounded just dandy."

"But what . . . ?"

"Turn that thing off a minute." Rachel did so. "Take your cassette out and stick this one in." Frances had produced one from a drawer above the record albums or scrapbooks. She handed it over. Rachel made the substitution and pushed the play button.

She heard the voice of a reporter covering some sort of outdoor event. It was obvious his activities were sponsored by American Airlines, for he was describing the flight he'd made nonstop from Chicago to New York in three hours, fifty-five minutes, and the connecting flight that had brought him to Lakehurst, New Jersey. As the commentary went on, it gradually dawned on Rachel what she was hearing, and she listened with fascinated horror. Across from her, Frances Payne had an excited, almost a sadistic expression on her face. She was nodding her head.

The voice said, "The ship is gliding towards us like some great feather, riding as though it's mighty proud of the place it's playing in the world's aviation . . ."

Rachel shook her head, as if willing not to happen what she knew was coming next. Frances Payne seemed to be getting a sick enjoyment from it.

"It's burst into flames!" the anguished voice on the tape said. Then he said something that sounded like "Get this, Scotty! Get this, Scotty! It's crashing, oh, it's crashing terribly . . ."

Rachel switched off the recorder.

"Had enough?" said Frances Payne, almost tauntingly. "There's more, you know."

"Yes, I'm sure. That poor man, having to see that and try to describe it. You—you were on board?"

128

"Yes I was. Later on he said, 'oh, the humanity, ladies and gentlemen,' and he says, there's 'not a possible chance of anybody being saved.' But I survived the *Hindenburg* all right. I showed them."

"You—showed them?"

"Oh, yes. You see, they blew that dirigible up just to kill me!"

16

RACHEL LOOKED ACROSS at the older woman's bloated face, not sure how to reply. Finally she said, "Do you really believe that?"

"You think I'm crazy, don't you?"

"No, but I think you might just be trying to frighten me."

"Am I succeeding?"

"Too well."

"If you don't want to hear any more of Herb Morrison's immortal broadcast, put *your* tape back in and I'll give you some more history." She said the word mockingly. "What does he call the *Hindenburg* on that tape? 'Some great feather,' isn't it? That's what memory is, Miss Hennings, a great feather on the wind that might blow anywhere at all."

Rachel changed the tapes with fingers that were maddeningly unsteady. When she was ready, Frances Payne continued to talk, matter-of-factly as though her dramatic introduction of the old news tape had never happened.

"I boarded the *Hindenburg* at Frankfurt. They brought us all to the airfield in buses and put us through a complete luggage search before we could board. They obviously suspected there would be some kind of sabotage, for I was told by others who'd traveled by zeppelin before that the thorough search was unusual. I remember we had to give up matches and lighters, and I was terrified I'd have to take a three-day journey without being able to smoke. There was a smoking room as it turned out, but it was closely guarded.

"The *Hindenburg* was magnificent, silvery in color and enormous as an ocean liner. It was raining as we boarded, and the stewards held umbrellas over our heads as we walked across the field to the ship. There were a number of Americans among the passengers, but surprisingly few women. I don't know why. You couldn't have gotten me in an airplane, but I didn't feel a moment's fear in the Hindenburg.

"They were giving the airship quite a send-off. This was its first transatlantic flight of 1937. There was a marching unit of Hitler Youth and a brass band playing 'Deutschland uber Alles.' It was quite magnificent really, and I was glad the studio had insisted. I didn't know what they had in store for me."

"The studio you worked for destroyed the *Hindenburg*?" Rachel ventured.

"You think I'm paranoid, just like Roger does. I don't say it *did* happen necessarily, but it *could* have happened. And there's something I've never been able to explain. I don't remember much about the catastrophe at Lakehurst. Mercifully, I guess. I remember seeing the skyline of New York. I remember passing over the field at Lakehurst and opening the windows—you could do that on a zeppelin—and looking down at the people below waiting to tie us up to the mooring mast. We'd have been very close to the ground then, just a couple hundred feet. I have no real memory of when the ship burst into flames—the flash of light and the burning, or of jumping to the ground when we were near enough, though that's the only way I could have escaped. I was in shock. I remember practically nothing of it at all. But when I came around, I was told by the representative of the studio who had flown out to get me that I shouldn't talk to the press about the fact that I was on board the *Hindenburg*'s last flight. Now, why wouldn't they want me to do that unless they were covering up the real reason for the explosion? If I talked, someone might realize I was the real target."

Rachel just shook her head.

"Oh, you don't have to believe me. I could never prove it, though I know there have been whole books about how the

Hindenburg was sabotaged for some small political reason."

"Why would anyone have wanted you dead? Enough so to go to all that trouble?"

"I knew a great deal too much about certain people in Hollywood, that's why. It's not dangerous information any more, but it would still be quite interesting, and eventually I hope to publish it. For a six-figure advance." For a moment, Frances Payne looked as if she were drifting off into a world of her own, forgetting Rachel was in the room. But suddenly, a new inspiration in her eye, she was back. "Want to know how I knew they didn't expect me to come back from Europe?"

"Yes, certainly."

"They sold my car out from under me. The car they bought me to drive around for publicity shots. I came back and it was gone."

"What kind of a car was it, Miss Payne?"

"A beautiful car. Red."

"And you say you worked for Americana Pictures?"

"That's right."

"Was the car a Duesenberg?"

"Why do you care what kind of a car I drove?"

"Well, you mentioned it."

"Just to show you how I knew they didn't expect me back alive, that's all."

"Did you know Wilbur DeMarco at all in Hollywood, Miss Payne?"

Her eyes narrowed. "Funny you should ask that. You know more than you would reveal, Miss Hennings."

"Do I?"

"He was one of them, one of the cadre of Commies and fellow travelers who tried everything to destroy the motion picture industry. Some of us did our best to root them out, and what did it get us? Blacklist, they screamed. Blacklist! Blacklist! What a sham, what a smokescreen. The real blacklist came from the left. People who believed in American ideals couldn't work in Hollywood after 1950. You ask Adolph Menjou. Oh, I know, you can't ask him—he's dead. But if you could have asked him, he could tell you. Do you think I wanted to retire from pictures? After 1950, I never got an offer, because nobody who identified herself with true Americanism could work. Blacklist! You tell me about blacklists."

Her little set piece about the *Hindenburg* had seemed calculated, but on this subject Frances Payne seemed genuinely out of control. Rachel asked, "Did you ever actually meet Wilbur DeMarco?"

"Oh, I don't know. I may have."

"What about Sally Jordan?"

"That bitch? She couldn't have played Scarlett O'Hara! They didn't even test her. Oh, her *politics* were the right color."

"Did you know her?"

"I didn't consort with that kind of people."

"Did you know Wilbur up here in Idyllwild?"

"Yes, but I never made the connection. He never said he was the same man, and they can fool you, they can be so charming. I never knew he was the same man. I'd have had nothing to do with him if I'd known."

"When did you find out?"

"I don't remember."

"Do you remember the car Wilbur DeMarco drove around Idyllwild?"

"No, I'm not very interested in cars really."

"Why did you son Roger show up at Wilbur's garage sale that morning?"

"Roger does what he wants."

"Wasn't he there at your behest? Did Wilbur have something in that house you wanted?"

"How would I know? I was never in his house." She glared at Rachel. "Who sent you here?" She was getting shrill. "Are you really after Roger or are you after something else?"

"I'm not after . . ."

"You can have Roger. I don't need Roger. And I'm not giving you what I know for nothing. I'll get a six-figure advance, and I'll write it all down, every bit of it."

Rachel was afraid she was losing her subject completely, but she made one last try. "Did you know William Klingsburg when you were in Hollywood? The muralist?"

"Oh, yes, no wonder he was a muralist. That man had twenty hands. Why didn't Congress ever investigate painters? It was always actors and writers and directors, but some of those painters really needed investigating. Most of them queer as Confederate money but get one that wasn't and you couldn't turn your back on him for a second." She leaned forward. "You still can't, you know. Don't trust him. He'll grab your ass and get paint all over it."

Rachel switched off the recorder. "I think it's time I went, Miss Payne. Thank you for talking with me." She stood up and walked to the door. As soon as she opened it, she saw Roger facing her. He was looking sad.

"I'll see you in a little while, mom," he said gently.

"You don't have to come back, Roger," Frances Payne said gratingly. "Go away with her, and stay away."

Roger closed the door and led Rachel out to his pickup without speaking. "You look a little shaky," he said.

"You didn't really warn me . . ."

"I thought it was one of her good days. I guess it wasn't as good a day as I thought. I guess we better give you a rain check on that dinner, huh?"

"Yes, I think so. Roger, does your mother ever leave the house?"

"It's been years."

"Are you sure of that?"

"I watch her rather closely. You can imagine why. But if I ever had to leave her, Rachel, there's plenty of money for a nurse. I don't have to stay here."

"It must be very hard on you."

"It's amazing what you can get used to. And she's not always that bad. I never would have brought you here if I thought she was going to go off like that."

"Roger, why did you come to Wilbur DeMarco's garage sale? Did she send you? Did she want something he had?"

"No, nothing special. She didn't send me. I was just kind of curious. I'd have liked to find out if that terrific old Duesenberg was in the sale, and how much he wanted for it, though it wouldn't be as practical as my truck." He smiled. "When I saw you there, I just had to stick around. Rachel, why don't you take me away from all this?"

"You could leave her?"

"Sure, like a shot."

"You'd be like the girl who gets married to get away from her family, Roger. Better get settled somewhere on your own first, before you start establishing any other relationships."

"I don't think you're offering to wait for me, are you?"

Tired of the subject, Rachel said, "Roger, tell me this. Was your mother really a passenger on the *Hindenburg*?"

"Got off on that, did she? Everything she knows about the *Hindenburg* is out of books or off that morbid tape she bought a couple years ago. She had a complete mental breakdown in 1937, and she spent most of the year in an institution. The studio did one monumental job of keeping it hushed up. Anything that was on the radio in the first half of that year she imagines herself an intimate part of. The other story's more fun—the one where she rejected the Prince of Wales and he hooked up with Mrs. Simpson on the rebound. You'll have to come back and hear that one some time."

"No, thanks," Rachel said.

"Oh, and she's positive she was aced out of Scarlett O'Hara by studio politics."

"What brought on your mother's breakdown? Do you know?"

"I obviously wasn't around then."

"But you knew she was institutionalized. Don't you know why?"

Before Roger could answer, they were interrupted. Jud Crompton's Buick pulled up in front of the house, stopping inches from the rear bumper of Roger's truck. Roger drew his breath in sharply, and Rachel was sure Jud had come as close as he did just to irritate the immaculate truck's owner.

"Say, now, you two are an item, aren't you?" Jud said jovially. "I see you together one more time and I'm gonna start a rumor."

Not replying to the statement, Roger merely said, "Not today, Jud."

"What do you mean?"

"You can't see her today."

"Well, I think your mom should be able to tell me for herself if she doesn't want to talk to me."

"She's not feeling well, Jud. You come back another day. Call first, maybe."

Jud turned to Rachel. "Did you meet Miss Payne, Rachel? Been interviewing her for your article?"

Rachel said, "Roger's right, Jud. I think I must have overtired her. She really isn't well."

Jud Crompton shrugged. "Well, I'm sure not going to force myself on somebody who's sick. But, Roger, I sometimes think you just don't want me to see her. And you know, she and I are both responsible adults, and if we have business to do, you're not going to stop us from doing it."

"I wouldn't dream of it, Jud," Roger said wearily. "But not today."

"Jud," Rachel said, "could you possibly give me a ride back into town? I don't think Roger should leave his mother at the moment."

"I'll be glad to."

Roger obviously didn't like the idea, but there wasn't much he could say about it. "I guess Rachel's right about that. Thanks very much, Jud. And Rachel, we'll keep in touch, won't we?"

"Of course, Roger," she said, and climbed into the Buick's passenger seat.

"Where should I drop you, Rachel?" Jud drove the mountain roads at a more stately pace than Roger Payne had.

"Your office is fine. I'll pick up one of those trail maps you promised me and walk back home."

"Fine. Old lady having one of her spells, was she?"

"What do you know about her spells, Jud?"

"That sounded kind of belligerent."

"I didn't mean it to be. I just want to know. What does the town know about Frances Payne?"

"The town doesn't see much of her."

"I know that, but . . . I'm not sure she's fully competent to manage her affairs."

Jud looked at her. "Fully competent? Oh, she's competent enough all right."

"It's in your interest that she be competent, isn't it, Jud?"

"We have some business pending, yes. But I surely wouldn't want to take advantage of somebody I thought was *non compos mentis*. What makes you think she's not all there?"

Rachel shook her head. "I've probably said enough. Her land out at Meditation Point must be worth a lot of money, huh?"

"Rachel, what do our local real-estate transactions have to do with you?"

"I don't know. Maybe I want to buy some property up here some time."

"If you want to buy DeMarco's house . . ."

"No, I don't mean to live in. For investment purposes. There must be a lot of development possibilities."

Jud said carefully, "People up here are kind of wary of development."

"So I've heard. You have to proceed with caution, don't you?"

"Compared to real estate, the book business is cut-and-dried, Rachel. I think you're still learning that business. Better get it down before you look into any other."

Keeping her voice light, she said, "Why that menacing note in your voice, Jud?"

"Menacing note? No such thing. Sorry if I gave you that impression. What I'm working on out at Meditation Point is no secret. I'm sure our friend young Roger would tell the whole wide world if they didn't know already. I'm as much of an environmentalist as anybody up here, Rachel, just as concerned about the plants and the animals, and, yeah, the people, too. But let me ask you something about Meditation Point. Ever try to meditate out there at sunset? Every damn time, there'll be some car full of kids playing rock music so loud old Tacquitz'd need earmuffs. Could you enjoy a sunset under those conditions? People get all sentimental about Meditation Point like it's some kind of a treasure. Sometimes I think it's just a menace to everybody's eardrums, if you want to talk about menacing."

"All I am is curious, but the way you reacted, I almost thought I was getting too close to something I wasn't supposed to know."

Jud brought the car to a jolting halt in front of Acorn Realty. He turned to her with a forced grin. "Sorry about that rough landing. I guess *I* was getting too close to something. It's just been a hard day, that's all. For you, too, if you had to deal with Frances Payne. I can't agree she's crazy, but I'll sure agree she's difficult. Come on in and get that map."

17

WHEN RACHEL WALKED out of the real-estate office, trail map in hand, she met Gil Franklin, who looked both concerned and angry. "Rachel, where the dickens have you been?"

"You didn't have an afternoon interview set for me, so I—"

"What good am I to you if you don't let me know where you are all the time? That was the whole point. You're dealing with some delicate matters here, and Stu is expecting me to watch out for you."

She laughed. "That brings back memories. The first time I met Stu, he'd been assigned by another guy to 'watch out for me.' Stu did such a good job, we wound up—well, closer friends than the other guy had anticipated."

Gil grinned in spite of himself. "Unlike Stu's, my intentions are strictly honorable. At my age, what choice do I have? I don't want anything to happen to you, though."

"I don't need an around-the-clock bodyguard, Gil. If I say I worry about your driving, you call me an ageist, and yet you expect me to act like some kind of fragile hothouse plant. I appreciate your help, don't get me wrong, but I can perform most functions for myself."

"You're dealing with a murder, Rachel—and probably a murderer. Will you tell me where you've been? Not as bodyguard but as assistant sleuth."

"If I do, you'll probably think I'm both stupid *and* in need of protection. But in my own defense, note that I'm still in one piece. Come on back to the house, and I'll heat us up some chili."

Over their second bowl, Rachel finished the account of her afternoon. Gil shook his head sadly. "I always wondered if Frances Payne had some kind of mental problem, but I just didn't want to believe it. It puts Roger in a spot—he obviously doesn't want to have her declared incompetent, but he doesn't want her to go in on this deal with Jud Crompton, either."

"Gil, she hated Wilbur. It wasn't just what she said. It was her whole demeanor, the look in her eye."

"You think she could have killed him, Rachel?"

"Who knows? I don't have an idea why. But she's obviously very unstable. And paranoid. If she did kill Wilbur, maybe it could explain why Roger Payne came to the garage sale. To find or destroy some evidence maybe, to cover up her crime. He said himself he wanted to have a look at Wilbur's Duesenberg. And I think that Duesenberg may have been a car that Frances Payne drove in 1937. Stu traced it to her old studio, Americana Pictures."

Gil shook his head. "But why would Wilbur have wanted to acquire her old car? And I can't imagine you're right about Roger. He seems like a straight enough kid to me."

"Gil, he once said to me not to worry, that he was no Norman Bates. Now why would he say that? Isn't that an odd thing to say? Unless he really *was* a Norman Bates."

"Too bad Wilbur's not around to solve his own murder. He'd have loved this plot."

Rachel had been deflecting barbs all week, but that one hit its mark and she flared out at him. "If I'm just playing whodunit parlor games, Gil, why are you and Stu so worried about me?"

"No matter what kind of crazy speculations you come up with, Rachel, we know Wilbur was really murdered. We saw him lying there in his own blood. And when you stir things up, you don't know what you might uncover. Maybe the last thing you're looking for."

"Exactly. What's on my schedule for tomorrow?"

"Well, now. Regarding Charles Freeman, I have good news and bad news. I know where he lives, but he won't see you under any circumstances."

"Did you see him?"

"No, he wouldn't open the door for me. He said he never sees anybody. His phone number is unlisted, and he doesn't give that to anybody. But he did say he would call you here tonight and talk about things over the phone."

"Hmmm. I wonder if Adam Kane has been to see him. He'd have to talk to him."

"Why would he have been? Adam's not pursuing our line of investigation at all. He's looking for a kid junkie, remember?"

"What's Freeman's address, Gil?"

"Rachel, that place doesn't look it, but it's as well guarded as Fort Knox. I was lucky I didn't get shot at by one of his people. I don't think you ought to go there."

"I didn't say I was going there. I just asked you for the address. Gil, if you're going to keep information from me, just tell me what you think's good for me—"

"Oh, simmer down. I'll tell you whatever you want to know. It happens, though, I *do* have enough interviews to keep you busy the next couple of days. Nobody from the Hollywood circle, you understand, but I think you ought to interview a few ordinary people just to make it look good, don't you?"

"Of course."

"I guess Stu's coming up for the weekend, huh?"

"Yes. I think we're going to try the Deer Springs Trail if the weather stays nice."

"Is Stu a hiker?"

"I'm going to find out."

The phone rang shortly after eight o'clock. Gil had gone home to his 1987 house, complete with satellite dish, to pick among several midwestern baseball games, and Rachel was contemplating the itinerary of a 1937, $18-per-day world cruise. She picked up the receiver on the first ring.

"Hello."

"Is this Miss Rachel Hennings?" A faded, elderly, but precise male voice.

"Yes. Are you Mr. Freeman?"

"That is correct. Miss Hennings, at the risk of seeming ungracious, I have to decline to participate in the research Mr. Franklin described to me. I am not in good health, and it requires all my energy to get myself through the day. I have had notoriety in my time, enough to last several lifetimes, and I would be extremely appreciative if you did not press me on this point. I do hope you understand."

"Yes, I do, Mr. Freeman, and I wouldn't want to involve you in anything that might endanger your health or bring you pain. But I should point out there may be more at stake here than just a magazine article."

There was a moment of silence at the other end. "I'm not surprised. Speak plainly, Miss Hennings. I've spent and given away more money in my time than most men will ever see, but I still have ample funds to effectuate my desires. Tell me what it is you want."

"Mr. Freeman, I don't quite understand. Are you offering to buy me off?"

"I would not take that step, Miss Hennings, until I had reason to think there was something to buy."

"I don't want any of your money, Mr. Freeman. Answer me a few simple questions, and I'll do my best not to bother you again."

"Ask your questions. I'll answer them if I can."

Rachel found herself stuck on where to go from there. She probably *was* going to bring this man pain, and judging by his voice, he was neither strong nor well. Still, she had to go ahead.

"Mr. Freeman, in 1937, you were married to an actress named Sally Jordan."

A sharp intake of breath. "Yes," he said softly.

"She didn't share your views on everything."

"On anything, Miss Hennings," he said, a note of gentle amusement in his voice. "To put it simply, she held views that in anyone else I regarded as nothing short of sedition. Hanging offenses. *My* opinions were—still are, in fact—so jingoistic and reactionary she couldn't be in the same room with anyone *else* who held them. Each of us favored books and opinion journals the other would cheerfully have burned. And yet we fell in love and married and got along famously for a while. A situation made possible by young and apolitical bodies, I suppose, biological functions that knew no voting booth. I like to think it was more than that, but it wasn't going to last . . ."

"Mr. Freeman, the reason I bring this up is . . . well, Mr. DeMarco, who died a few days ago, knew your wife rather well."

"Yes, rather well."

"Do you know how they met?"

"At some sort of political meeting. I remember Sally came home in a terrible state afterwards, a bundle of nerves."

"Mr. DeMarco had that much of an effect on her?"

"Not exactly." Freeman sounded amused. "I believe they witnessed a traffic accident after leaving the meeting. I think there was a fatality involved. I might have hoped associating DeMarco with that event might discourage her interest in him, but it didn't work out that way."

"Do you know anything else about this traffic accident?"

"No. She was in no condition to discuss it the night she came home, and after that, I never wanted to mention it again."

"She was never called upon to testify about it in court or anything like that?"

"No, the matter never came up again."

"What do you remember about Mr. DeMarco in 1937?"

"Miss Hennings, I never met Wilbur DeMarco in my life.

But at the time of my wife's tragic death in New York, she and I were in the process of getting a divorce. She loved this DeMarco and wanted to marry him. I wanted her with me more than anything I owned, but I was wise enough to know I couldn't own her, and I was not disposed to stand in the way of her happiness. I have to admit I hated DeMarco without knowing him, while recognizing how illogical that is. For all I knew about him was that he shared my wife's misguided politics, which I could readily forgive in her, and that he was under the spell of her beauty and charm, which I could readily forgive in myself. But human nature doesn't work logically, does it?"

"Then you never met Wilbur DeMarco here in Idyllwild either?"

"Never. I can say that quite confidently, because I have met no one in Idyllwild. I have two servants who do everything for me that involves leaving the house. The brief conversation I had with your friend Mr. Franklin this afternoon was one of only a handful of examples of Charles Freeman's social intercourse in this mountain community, and the first in about five years. When you're rich as I am, Miss Hennings, you can almost make yourself invisible—not totally, I guess, because someone obviously tipped you off I was here."

"William Klingsburg, the painter," Rachel said, feeling no reluctance about naming her source in this instance.

"Yes, I should have known. I bought some paintings from him a few years ago. In matters of art as in matters of sexuality, Miss Hennings, I am able to look past politics. That ability brought me Sally for a too-brief time and has brought me some beautiful things to look at. Now, is there anything else I can help you with?"

"Not at the moment."

"Not at any other moment, let me warn you now."

"What do you think happened to your wife, Mr. Freeman? Who do you think killed her?"

"Of course I've thought about it over and over, but I just

don't know. And neither did the police. A petty thief, perhaps. Possibly a political crime? She must have provoked some enemies with her radical activities. But there was nothing to lead the police to her killer."

"Where were you when she died, Mr. Freeman?"

"I was in New York, as it happened. But we were apart by then. The police questioned me, of course, but I was able to satisfy them I was miles from Times Square. I could probably also provide an alibi for the death of Wilbur DeMarco, but I don't really expect that to be necessary, do you?"

"When you bought the paintings from Mr. Klingsburg, did you know he had known your wife?"

"He didn't mention it, but if you've met the man, you know he speaks in some kind of code. I've never been able to talk to artists except with my eye."

"How do you spend your time now, Mr. Freeman, if you don't mind my asking?"

"If I don't mind—my dear young woman, that's the least personal question you've asked and the one I am most happy to answer. I am writing a definitive history and analysis of the Communist conspiracy in the United States, and when you read it, you'll see that the late Mr. Robert Welch didn't go nearly far enough."

18

THE NEXT TWO days' interviews were enjoyable enough, but the four subjects—one of whom had actually lived in Idyllwild since 1937 and knew local lore inside out—had no direct knowledge of Wilbur DeMarco except as a pleasant man they occasionally saw around town or at the mailboxes. It seemed to Rachel that Gil kept producing these safe interview subjects just to keep her from going off on any dangerous tangents, so Thursday and Friday became a sort of vacation from her ulterior motive of murder investigation. Rachel wasn't unduly frustrated, since she expected to spend at least one more week, and she considered her progress to date even more substantial than she had hoped. Talking to more of the local seniors was a pleasurable way to kill time until she got a look at Wilbur DeMarco's unfinished manuscript.

On Thursday night, Stu called with the news that he'd received DeMarco's manuscript from Hannah Spurgeon via express mail and would be bringing it up with him the following evening. But he had more to report. "It's not just the manuscript. There's a handwritten letter from Wilbur to Hannah dated January 10, 1938."

"You have to read it to me."

"Okay. Here goes. 'Dear Hannah, Thanks for your patience. I want to finish the book, not because I have any enthusiasm left for it, but because I like to think of myself as some kind of a professional. I'll give myself another month, and if I can't do it, I'll return the check. That may not be very satisfactory, but it beats drinking the money away and not

146

producing a script either. I'm at a low ebb at the moment. Maybe it will get better, but then again I don't see how. I went to a party at a producer's house out here New Year's Eve. All the old gang there but the one who mattered. I was drinking and miserable without knowing they were the last happy hours of my life. She called me a little after nine, speaking to me from '1938' in Times Square, wishing me Happy New Year. I was lonesome and drank some more. I heard what had happened when I woke up the next day, and my whole life shattered on me, little pieces everywhere. Thanks for letting me cry on your shoulder, Hannah. I am going to try to finish the book, though I think it has to be Henry Friday's swan song. His kind of games will never be fun to me again. No need to tell anybody what you know about me and Sally—I don't want to embarrass poor old Freeman, who must have loved her, too. With thanks and affection, as ever, Wilbur."

Stu couldn't see the tear making its way down Rachel's cheek, but she betrayed it with a loud snuffle. Stu didn't say anything but waited for her. As he'd expected, her first remark was all business.

"Stu, Hannah knows more than she told me when we talked on the phone. She claimed she didn't even know what Wilbur's real-life crime was."

"Maybe she forgot and finding the letter refreshed her memory."

"I doubt that. I don't think she forgets anything."

"She was probably just following Wilbur's original instructions then. And I guess now she's decided to trust you a little more. She certainly wants you to know. I can't imagine a copy of this letter was included by accident."

"She wanted more than thanks and affection from Wilbur, according to his cousin. Now she's talking about getting his books back in print."

"Nothing like getting murdered to restore your literary fortunes."

"I think it means more to her than that. Have you read any of the manuscript yet?"

"A little. It's about—"

"Don't tell me anything. I want to come to it with an unprejudiced eye. Write down your impressions, and we can discuss them on our way up to Suicide Rock on Saturday. I have some other ideas to share with you, too. About Wilbur's car and—"

"Our way to where? Rachel, I'm very fond of you, but that's a big step to take."

"After the first step, there's nothing to it. You'll enjoy it, Stu. I'll get us a wilderness permit in town tomorrow."

"Wilderness permit? Why do we need a wilderness permit?"

"So they can account for people who go into the wilderness, I guess."

"And why do they have to account for them? Because they don't always come back, right? Rachel, that very word wilderness has ominous overtones."

"Sure, you don't see me going up there during the week, do you? I need a protector. Gil's been protecting me from murderers all week. The least you can do is ward off the lions and tigers and bears for one morning."

"Uh, let's talk about it when I get there. We may want to sleep in or something."

"We'll have plenty of time for 'or something' and a hike. I'm getting cabin fever, Stu."

"Oh, by the way, I talked to that kid who's watching the bookstore for you. He sold a Shakespeare first folio for forty-nine cents and paid four hundred bucks for a set of Judith Krantz first editions."

"If he did, he used his own money. It won't work, Stu."

"In the window, he's featuring three hundred Harlequin Romances with ripped covers."

"See you tomorrow, Stu."

148

The following evening, they celebrated Stu's arrival by having dinner at the Gastrognome. Everything on the plates and in the glasses was first-rate, and the roaring fire encouraged mellowness on the chilly night, but throughout the meal Stu could tell Rachel was on edge, itching to get the formalities of eating finished and race back to the DeMarco house. And he realized she was lusting not after his slender white body but the hundred pages of Wilbur DeMarco's manuscript.

When she had settled down with it, Stu worried away at their own fire for a while, took down a pristine first American edition of A.J. Cronin's *The Citadel* with the idea of comparing it with the TV serial, admired Rachel's trim ankles crossed over an ottoman, and generally concentrated on not bothering her.

Fortunately, she was a fast reader, and he knew that at the rate she was whipping through the photocopied pages, it wouldn't take her long to finish it.

Rachel knew Wilbur DeMarco's style pretty well by now, and there was no doubt this was the real thing. He did seem to be spending a little more energy on developing his characters, but the book wasn't quite the breakthrough Hannah Spurgeon had implied.

The setting was, as expected, Hollywood. Henry Friday, whose usual base of operations was New York, had been asked by an old friend, playwright Trevor Dawson, to investigate a delicate problem: a social-action organization called Justice Unlimited, which had been formed to provide a defense for people wrongly accused of crimes, was experiencing a mysterious drain on its resources. It seemed someone in the organization was diverting funds to his (or her) own benefit, but Dawson didn't know how it was being done. After Friday had met all the members of the organization, an amusing cross section of movieland types, his friend Dawson was found clubbed to death with a croquet mallet in his study, all doors and windows firmly locked from

149

the inside. Wilbur had not renounced his classical roots.

Since playwright Dawson had been given most of the good lines, the story bogged down a bit after the murder. When Wilbur seemed to be getting it off the ground again with some good interrogation of the suspects, the fragment ran out in the middle of a chapter.

Rachel turned the last page of the photocopy at a little after ten o'clock. Stu looked across at her for a while, enjoyed the fire reflected in her eyes, and waited for her to say something.

"That was a unique experience," she said finally.

"And a useful one?"

"I think so, but it'll take some mulling over."

"Is it really better than Wilbur's other books?"

"No, Hannah Spurgeon probably overrated it. I'm not so sure it could have been published even if Wilbur had finished it."

"I didn't think it was that bad."

"It isn't bad at all, but it's too much of a roman à clef. There are people I know in this book, and if they're recognizable after fifty years, they must have been even more so then. And I think the plot was based on reality, too. This do-gooder organization that Henry Friday is working for sounds an awful lot like the group he was in with Sally Jordan, the Committee for Freedom and Justice. Of course, in the book, the organization isn't as overtly political as the real-life group—unlike helping the Loyalists in Spain, defending the wrongfully accused was a goal that any reader should be able to identify with, regardless of politics. And, Stu, didn't you tell me the Committee for Freedom and Justice disbanded in 1938 over a missing-funds scandal? Just like the one plaguing Wilbur's fictional organization?"

"I don't know about 'just like,' but yes, I noticed the similarity, too. So you think the Dawson character is based on Wilbur himself? Weirdly prophetic, since he's the murder victim. Or maybe he's based on Monte Fanning, the guy who killed himself."

"That would be just as weird, since Fanning was still alive when Wilbur wrote this. I think Wilbur more or less saw himself in the role of Dawson. Certainly he provides Dawson all the best wisecracks. Fanning we don't know, but Wilbur must have known him and he *might* be a character in the book. There's another writer in the story who's a close friend of Dawson's. But what's the use of speculating about that?"

"Right. Give me an example of one of these characters you're sure was drawn from life."

She turned over a few sheets, looking for an especially obvious instance. "Take this bit:

> "What about you, Mr. Ortega?" Friday asked. "Did you see Forbes give Oglesby the money?"
>
> "Money," the sculptor said contemptuously. "Bad art. What is money to Ortega?"
>
> "Well, it can be used to buy good art," Friday pointed out.
>
> "Proves the point," cracked Dawson. "What is money to Ortega?"

"Very bright dialogue," Stu said, "Klingsburg, no?"

"Yes. His physical description, his medium, his ethnicity are all different, but he talks just like Klingsburg. Look, here's another example.

> "To what lady do I give the honor of Ortega's attentions tonight? Come with me, Griselda. I have not experienced dancing with a tall redhead."

"Dancing?" Stu said incredulously.

"This is the '30s. Mystery novels were rather conservative in those days, Wilbur's kind anyway, and dancing was a kind of metaphor for sex. Archie Goodwin did a lot of dancing, you might remember. I have a hunch I know who Griselda is based on, too."

"Really? Who?"

"Hannah Spurgeon."

"His editor? Putting her in the book seems a little risky. Do you think she recognized herself?"

"I seriously doubt it. Griselda in the book is a six-foot amazon who makes Henry Friday's life miserable by her overattentiveness to him. Friday, of course, was a committed bachelor along the lines of Philo Vance. The way Griselda throws herself at him is a source of comedy. That, according to his cousin, is how Wilbur saw Hannah Spurgeon, though certainly not how she saw herself. Besides, Griselda is a press agent, not an editor, and he made her the exact physical opposite of Hannah, who I understand is under five feet, though she certainly sounded taller on the phone.

"And here's another character, the young actor John Forbes. Catch the dialogue here:

> "Gee, Mr. Friday, I'd be in a heck of a jam if my family found out I was doing anything like this. To my father, suggesting the D.A. could ever accuse an innocent person is kinda like rooting for the Indians against the Cavalry."
>
> Friday smiled encouragingly. "Your family doesn't need to find out, Mr. Forbes. That is, if you've told me the truth."
>
> Forbes laughed nervously. "I'm not a good enough actor to lie."

"John Forbes isn't an ex-Olympic athlete, but that character's obviously based on Jack Hooper. Wilbur gave Forbes Jack Hooper's speech patterns. Hooper says things like 'kinda' and 'a heck of a' incessantly. And his family really would have objected if they thought he was involved in an organization like the Committee for Freedom and Justice."

"But you said Hooper denied he had any kind of political involvement and said he didn't think he'd ever met Wilbur."

Rachel nodded slowly. "He was lying, Stu. This makes it

obvious. I probably should have suspected it sooner. He was so insistent he didn't remember meeting Wilbur in his Hollywood days. Then when I whipped out that poster, proving he'd been in one of the Henry Friday films, he backtracked a little and said maybe he had after all but he'd been in so many movies that year, he couldn't keep them straight. Looking back on our conversation, it seems so obvious he was hiding something. I'll have to talk to Jack Hooper again, I think."

"Wait a second. Don't you think you ought to tell that sheriff's deputy what you know?"

"Too soon. We're just playing games as far as he's concerned. I want to have enough solid information that he won't just laugh in my face. And this isn't the only lead I have, you know."

"It isn't?"

"No. I've developed a whole different theory with a whole different cast of characters."

"All on your own, huh?"

"Oh, no, with some of the information I got from you." She told him about her conversations with Frances Payne and Charles Freeman.

Stu nodded his head periodically and finally said, "Okay, but what does it all add up to?"

"Consider this little train of reasoning. We know Frances Payne had a mental breakdown early in 1937, but we don't know what brought it on. We also know that the night they first met Wilbur and Sally witnessed a fatal traffic accident—"

"We don't know that. It could have just been what Sally told Freeman."

"Okay, we don't know it for sure, but hear me out. They witnessed a traffic accident, but after that night it was never heard of again. Sally never had to testify. Sounds like a cover-up, right? And who had the power to cover up an event like that in Hollywood? A major movie studio, like Americana Pictures. And on whose behalf might they want to cover it up? A star like Frances Payne. I think Frances either had a collision and caused another driver's death or ran over and killed a pedestrian. I think she wasn't too mentally stable to begin with, and the anguish of the accident pushed her over the edge. The studio had the accident hushed up with police cooperation, spirited Frances away to a mental hospital, and got rid of the car, the 1936 Duesenberg that Wilbur was able to acquire years later."

"I suppose it's possible."

"It fits the facts. And maybe Frances came around from her mental illness, remembered the whole story, and realized that Sally and Wilbur were witnesses, perhaps unfriendly ones, to her guilt in the accident. Maybe she was in New York on New Year's Eve. Maybe she killed Sally."

"Nothing to prove it."

"Of course not. But more to the point, maybe Wilbur *thought* she could have killed Sally. Maybe he acquired the old Duesenberg, a car Dorie Moss said he didn't really like, in order to smoke out Frances. We couldn't figure out why he would acquire one unauthentic item, a 1936 car in his 1937 collection. But maybe the one apparently unauthentic item was really the one *truly authentic* item, a relic of an actual 1937 event, the real car involved in Frances Payne's accident. Maybe that was his 1937 crime, not Sally Jordan's death. He first drove the Duesenberg on the streets of Idyllwild about three years ago, and that was about the same time Frances Payne became such a determined recluse. Maybe seeing the car was what forced her into her hole, not her objection to paying for her own spaghetti."

"She killed Wilbur, too?"

"If she killed Sally, I'll bet she killed Wilbur. But of course, we don't know. There's lots more investigating to do, Stu."

Stu sighed with mock resignation. "I guess we'll be too busy for that hike tomorrow, huh?"

"And waste a perfectly good wilderness permit? Not on your life."

19

IT WAS A cool morning, but Stu Wellman was starting to sweat. Rachel was a few yards ahead of him, forming as pleasant a part of the view as the chipmunks and manzanita, but this was a steep trail, and Stu was a city person. Rachel seemed to be having a great time, but she was unencumbered, and Stu had their lunch and other essential belongings in the pack on his back. Finally, he saw her go off the trail to a clearing atop a large rock. He followed her with a sense of relief.

"Isn't this view magnificent?" she said, gesturing to the expanse of trees, mountains, and blue sky.

"Sure, sure." He managed to shrug off the pack and sit down beside her on the rock. "So we're finally here, huh?"

Rachel looked at him. "Finally here? We're just getting started. We haven't even entered the wilderness yet."

"This isn't Suicide Rock?"

"Stu, we've been walking less than half an hour. Did you think we had to pack a lunch just to come up here?"

"So we don't eat yet, huh?"

"It's not even ten o'clock."

"I think this mountain atmosphere does something to my time sense."

"Actually, Jud Crompton told me the first stretch up to the viewpoint is about the hardest part of the hike. It'll be more fun from here on."

"Only if it's downhill." Stu looked over his shoulder. "Say, we have company."

Alice Zimmer, the legs that were her best feature bare and

brown, was walking over to where they sat. "Well, hi, Rachel!"

Stu started to say, "Aren't you—?"

"Alice, this is Stu Wellman. He was at the Town Prom but I don't think you actually met."

"Well," Stu said, "we weren't formally introduced, but . . ."

"This is Alice Zimmer, Stu. One of my new Idyllwild friends. Are you on your way up or down, Alice?"

"Oh, down. I like to get an early start. Jud was supposed to hike up with me, but he had to go into Hemet again. I don't know what it is with that man. He's working on some kind of a deal, and he's just like a horse with the bit in his teeth. Or maybe I mean a horse that's thrown the bit out of his teeth. I'm not sure."

"Are there very many people on the trail?"

"I just met one or two. You know, you hardly ever see town people on the trails up here. It's mostly the tourists. I can't remember when I last met somebody I actually knew. Most Idyllwild people get on the trails about as often as people who live in Anaheim go to Disneyland. Jud and I are different, though. We try to do one of the hikes every weekend when we can."

"How much farther is it to Suicide Rock?" Stu asked.

"Oh, a couple of miles. You just visiting, Stu?"

"Yeah, I'm what you call a flatlander. And getting more confirmed in my flatlandedness every minute. Is the rest of the way all uphill?"

She smiled. "Well, mostly. But just imagine how easy it'll be to come down."

"Any snow up in the wilderness?" Rachel asked.

"Quite a few patches still. The trail is clear, though."

"Do you ever get any fresh snow in town this time of year?"

"It's unusual, but it's been known to happen. I think we're safe for a few days."

"What time did you start out this morning?" Stu asked.

156

"Around seven."

"Aren't you cold?"

Alice glanced at her bare thighs with obvious pride of ownership. "No. I think you guys are a little overdressed actually. It can get pretty warm."

Rachel shivered. "That's hard to believe. What's Jud working on in Hemet? Any idea?"

Alice shrugged. "I never know about his big deals till he pulls one off. Then he tells me all about it. It makes me feel easier when I know people like Jud are working in real estate up here—you know, people who have a real concern for the environment."

With studied casualness, Stu said, "I've heard rumors somebody wants to build houses at Meditation Point."

"So have I, believe me. Rachel and I talked about it. Have you been up there, Stu?"

"Oh, yeah, it's beautiful."

"It's a public treasure. And as for this development talk, I don't think it'll ever happen, though I really can't blame Jud for wanting to make the deal, if the deal has to be made."

Rachel asked, "Any idea who owns the land?"

"Different people, I think," she said vaguely.

"It doesn't do them much good, sitting there unused, does it, even if it is a public treasure."

"That's the way Jud feels. What is it producing for the owners of the property?"

"Maybe they should put up a toll booth or something," Stu offered.

"I don't expect anything *that* crass. Actually, I think most of the owners live nearby. So they're protecting their own views by not allowing any development there. In the long run, it's probably worth it to them, and they'd get the money back if they ever sold their own places."

"What if one of the owners decided to sell?" Rachel said. "What could the others do about it?"

"I think they'd just get together and pool their funds to

buy the property. I know the people up here, Rachel—the good people anyway. They'd do anything to discourage development. In fact, that may be what Jud's really after, negotiating the sale from one landowner to another, so the development never takes place. I never thought of that till now, but that'd be typical of Jud. He's a concerned citizen. He really is."

"I'm sure you're right." Rachel got to her feet. "Well, Stu, if we want to get to Suicide Rock by lunchtime, we probably better get going."

Suppressing a groan, Stu also got up.

"I'm going to go by the shop," Alice said. "Officially, I give myself Saturday off, but you just can't trust hired help to do things your way, so I'd better look in and see what's happening. What do you think of these kids nowadays, Stu?"

Stu shook his head. "Don't ask me. I'm still a kid myself."

He watched her retreating form for a moment and told Rachel, "Your legs are as good as hers."

"If I bared them for you now, they'd have all the sex appeal of a freshly plucked Christmas turkey. Different metabolism, I guess."

"You and the blond menace are sure chummy. She has a lot of nerve assuming I'm part of her generation. I'm closer to your age than hers."

Rachel considered that. "Well, maybe halfway between. Come on, old-timer. Prove your youth by getting back on the trail."

"Sure, sure. Do you understand her relationship with Jud Crompton? She seems to try so hard to convince herself he's okay. Who was the character in Shakespeare who protested too much?"

"I think it was somebody going up Deer Springs Trail," Rachel said, giving Stu's shoulder a gentle shove. "Want to lead the way for a while?"

Stu shook his head. "Couldn't go fast enough for you, young'n. I'll lead coming down."

158

After another hour's climb, they came to a junction. Taking the trail that went off to the right, it would be just one more mile to Suicide Rock.

"See?" Rachel said. "Just another mile to go. Piece of cake."

"This is not quite like a mile in downtown L.A., Rachel."

"It sure isn't. The air's better, and the scenery's more interesting."

"And the sidewalk's steeper. How about some lunch?"

"Still too early."

"A drink then." Stu shrugged off the pack and took out one of the plastic water bottles. "What's Jud Crompton really up to, Rachel? He didn't strike me as the Sierra Club type, and there's more to it than Meditation Point."

"I think there's something he wants to keep Alice in the dark about. He's not making all these trips off the hill to look for Jack Finney first editions, I'm pretty sure of that."

"She's kidding herself about him. What do a pair like that see in each other?"

Rachel looked Stu over for a moment, a mock-critical expression on her face. From several angles, she took in his skinny frame, stooped posture, prominent beak, and martyred expression. Finally she said, "The ways of human attraction are mysterious indeed."

Caught for once without a comeback, Stu put back the water bottle, slung the pack back over his shoulders, and said, "Come on, let's go. Suicide Rock or bust."

Deer Springs Trail twisted and winded through the trees and rocks, climbing steadily. Rachel and Stu trudged along for another twenty minutes before stopping again, at his insistence. Rachel was about to kid him about needing another rest so soon, but when she turned, she saw something on Stu's face besides fatigue and long-suffering martyrdom.

"Stu, what . . . ?" He raised his hand to quiet her.

After a moment, he said in a muted voice, "I don't hear it

any more."

"Hear what?"

"Somebody's been following us. I could hear the crunching of the rocks behind us. You can't hear it because you're in the lead."

"It's a public trail, Stu," she said, but she kept her voice low. "Anybody can use it."

"I've been hearing it for quite a while now, and let's face it, Rachel, we're not fast hikers. I'm doing the best I can, but I sense you're under wraps."

"So there's another slow hiker on the trail."

Stu shook his head emphatically. "No, I tell you. I heard it before we even got to the junction, but I thought I was imagining it. He stops when we stop. Somebody back there's following us, and he won't show himself. I don't like that."

Rachel wanted to tell Stu he was being silly, but she knew his imagining things was not typical. Picking up threatening emanations was more her style. If Stu thought somebody was following them, he was probably right.

"What should we do?" she said, even more quietly. "Turn around and confront whoever it is?"

"Worth a try."

The footsteps seemed to be getting closer and closer. Then a friendly sounding voice said, "Hi, Rachel!"

It was Roger Payne, grinning broadly, dressed in state-of-the-art hiking boots and sexy shorts, unencumbered by a pack on his back. To an objective eye, he wouldn't look menacing, but in context, he could have been the Phantom of the Opera.

Rachel demanded in a strained voice, "Just what are you doing here?"

Stu said accusingly, "You've been following us all morning."

Roger smirked. "Us nothing. I've been following her."

Now amused in spite of herself, but fighting it, Rachel said, "Why don't you turn around and go back to your chores?"

160

Roger looked a little repentant for the first time. "I never did anything like this before, Rachel. Didn't have to. When I see you, or when I think of you, something comes over me."

"Something's gonna come over you if you don't get lost!" Stu's fists were clenched, and Rachel knew he was ready to fight for her, however outmanned he might be. She felt a little ashamed that this only increased her amusement.

"I'm going," Roger said, "but I have to tell you something first, Rachel. For one thing, I wanted to say I was sorry about the other day. Mom really isn't like that all the time, and if I'd known I'd be subjecting you to such an unpleasant experience..."

"Don't worry about that, Roger. I wanted to talk to her. I just hope my visit didn't upset her too much."

Roger drew in his breath. "I think she enjoyed herself. Hell, she thrives on it. She loves a chance to trot out her paranoia, and most of it relates to the past. In anything that's happening right now, she isn't crazy at all. She's made her deal with Jud Crompton on the Meditation Point property."

"Has she?"

"He was there last night. They did it all behind closed doors, didn't let me know what they were talking about. Like a couple of conspirators. He plays her like a fiddle when they're together. Knows just what to say. Not that I think he got the best of her, you understand."

"When she makes a financial deal, you're not in on it? She doesn't ask your advice or tell you what she's doing?"

He shook his head. "No, never. To her, I'm still just an ignorant kid. This time she was more secretive than ever, and the two of them looked like they'd really pulled something off. When I asked her if she'd made a deal with him, she smirked and said that deal was made months ago. If it was, I'd like to know why Jud Crompton kept on sniffing around. My mother *is* a good businesswoman, Rachel. She's never put a foot wrong in that respect. I suppose we'll see houses on Meditation Point now. But I have a feeling there's more

161

to it than that."

"Something dishonest, Roger?"

He smiled. "I didn't say that, but my mother gets a certain look in her eye. Well, I guess I've interrupted your day and made enough of a fool of myself. I'll go down the trail like a good boy."

"Wait a second before you go, Roger," Rachel said. Might as well bring this up now, when he was feeling somewhat on the defensive. "What do you know about that old Duesenberg Wilbur DeMarco owned?"

Roger looked nonplused. "Just that it was a beautiful old car."

"Did it have some kind of special significance for your mother?"

Roger looked wary now. "Why should it have?"

"Didn't she quit leaving her house about the time Wilbur DeMarco first drove it on the streets of Idyllwild?"

"I don't know. But if she did, it was just a coincidence."

"But didn't she ask you to go to Wilbur's garage sale to have a look at it, see it if was available for sale?"

"Well, yes, she did as a matter of fact."

"Do you know why?"

"No, I don't. I wondered."

"Your mother mentioned the car she'd driven before her supposed trip to Europe in 1937, didn't she?"

Roger looked convincingly surprised. "Was that the car?"

"Don't you know?"

"She never said what make it was. She was sure angry that they sold it out from under her, and of course, it fed her paranoia."

"But you don't know why the car was sold?"

He looked helpless. "Look, Rachel, I don't even know *if* the car was sold. I don't know if the car ever existed. I wasn't around then, and I never know just what to believe and not believe about that period. I don't want you to think my mother's crazy, but that whole period is a muddle in her

162

mind. It's all dukes and *Hindenburgs* and Scarlett O'Haras. She can never get it straight."

The three of them stood there for a moment, with nothing more to say. Finally Roger asked, "Can I go now? This wasn't the scene I had in mind."

"Go ahead, Roger," Rachel said distractedly.

He turned to walk away. "Don't think I'm giving up," he said cheerfully, as if trying to break the uncomfortable mood.

Stu watched the younger man's retreating form until it disappeared into the trees. Then he turned back to Rachel, and only when he saw her face did he realize how funny it all was and how surprisingly little resentment he felt toward Roger. The winner can afford to be generous.

To the amazement of them both, Stu and Rachel actually reached Suicide Rock, enjoyed the view and their lunch with self-congratulatory pleasure, and were back down to Stu's car, parked across highway 243 in the parking lot of the Idyllwild Visitors' Center, by three o'clock that afternoon.

"Aren't you proud of yourself?" Rachel said, as he drove back toward town.

"Oh, I guess a little. Shall we go back to the Gastrognome to celebrate? Of course, with my luck, young Roger will probably have signed on as a waiter."

"Don't you remember, Gil asked us over for dinner?"

"Doesn't he see enough of you during the week?"

"Stu, if you're going to be jealous of an eighty-year-old man . . ."

"It's quite a tribute to him. I'm just honoring my elders. Aren't you on to me, Rachel? I'm jealous of Gil and the movie star's pretty-boy son and the late Wilbur DeMarco and the whole lot of them."

As they pulled into the driveway of the DeMarco house, they saw a marked Riverside County Sheriff's vehicle parked out in front. Deputy Adam Kane was just walking back up the walk as they arrived.

"Afraid I'd missed you," he said. He was grim-faced but civil. "How are you, Mr. Wellman? Miss Hennings?"

"How's your investigation coming, Deputy?" Rachel asked.

"Not too bad. How's yours?"

"Mine? What do you mean?"

"Miss Hennings, I got a telephone call down at the office from some old woman in New York reading me out for not doing a better job on this case."

"That must have been Hannah Spurgeon," Rachel said.

"It was, and if that's so funny, I wish you'd let me in on the joke. I get enough flak just in Riverside County without nuisance calls from the East Coast."

"I didn't ask her to call you," Rachel said, controlling her amusement with an effort.

"I'm sure you didn't, but I'd like to know exactly what you're up to. It's not just some magazine article. Some of the people you've talked to have been telling me you're doing some kind of amateurish investigation into Wilbur De-Marco's death."

"Who told you that?"

"Never mind who. If that is what you're doing, I'd appreciate it if you'd cut it out."

Stu said, "Kane, what's the harm, really? She's not interfering with anything you're doing, and if she should happen to turn up something . . ."

"Mr. Wellman, it is not as simple a matter as you seem to think. Police-community relations are one of our biggest concerns, and I just can't have things going on that make it appear I'm not doing my job. I suppose you've been encouraging her in this."

Stu smirked. "Exactly the opposite, I think."

"Yeah, you and Gil Franklin, that old crank who's always sounding off about police protection on the hill. We do the best we can with what we have, and I can tell you it is *adequate* for the needs of a community like Idyllwild. But what

164

we don't have time to do in a tragic but simple murder investigation is get it off playing Charlie Chan." He turned to Rachel and added sarcastically, "Or Nancy Drew!"

Stu could have predicted the reaction. The name of the long-running juvenile heroine always pushed the wrong button with Rachel. Though she managed to restrain herself from blowing her top, her body language spoke volumes.

When Kane had left and they'd gone in the house, she was still steaming.

"He calls it a simple investigation, and I guess it is simple if you can't solve it. Not as much paperwork."

"Cool off, Rachel, he's a nice guy trying to do his job, and Hannah Spurgeon just rubbed him the wrong way."

"Sure, I know." She walked over to the table where the phone was and started rifling through the directory.

"What are you looking for?"

"Jack Hooper's number. There may be time to go see him before Gil expects us."

She turned the dial on Wilbur DeMarco's period phone and listened intently to the ringing on the other end. After a while, Stu said gently, "I think there's a seniors' track meet down at USC this weekend. You'll probably have to wait till Monday."

She set down the phone. "Why didn't Charlie Chan ever have this problem?"

Gil Franklin roared with laughter at the description of Rachel's encounter with Adam Kane. "Oh, I wish I'd'a been there. It's really my fault, Rachel. I've been complaining about police protection up here for years, and they all know me. The fact that I'm helping you out gave Adam the chance to vent how he feels about me on you. Can I refill those glasses?"

Rachel covered her brandy glass with a quick hand, but Stu accepted some more. Luckily they were going to be walking home, having had just enough strength left after their heroic hike to Suicide Rock to come to Gil's house on foot.

"But, Gil, who here in town do you think would have talked to him about my interviews? And what would be the point?"

"Oh, anybody might. Quite innocently. Nothing sinister about it. He might have talked to Dorie about something to do with finding Wilbur's body, and she might have mentioned it to him. She's a talkative lady and not too good about concealing things, you know. Anyway, why not? You didn't swear anybody to secrecy."

"I guess you're right."

"No harm done, is there?"

"No, I don't suppose."

Gil chuckled. "Oh, heck, Rachel, I know darn well it was Dorie. She said she mentioned your investigation to Kane and I told her in no uncertain terms she talks too much. Don't be mad at her, will you?"

"Of course not. Do I have any appointments for Monday, Gil?"

"Not yet, but I thought tomorrow I might line somebody up."

"Please don't. I have some other things I want to do on Monday."

Stu looked at her sharply. "Be sure to tell Gil where you're going."

"Or take me along," Gil said.

"I can take care of myself in broad daylight, thanks."

"Anything planned for tomorrow?"

"Stu's taking me down to Palm Springs for the day. And we might go to Indio and see if any of the date places are still in business."

Gil shook his head sadly. "They are, but it may not be long. Pretty soon you won't be able to tell Riverside County from L.A.—just one continuous city. Folks, when I first came out here, they still grew oranges in Orange County. Can you believe that?"

20

THE AGED RUNNER had his usual wide smile and friendly wave. Rachel had been walking toward town but she did a 360-degree turn and asked Jack Hooper if she could join him on his run. Luckily, she was properly shod for the activity.

"Why, sure," he said between breaths. "Best offer I've had in a long time."

She got into step next to him, letting him set the pace. "How was the meet yesterday?"

"Ran second. The guy that beat me's a kinda ringer, though. Just turned seventy last week. When I get to run with the eighty-year-olds, I'm gonna be dynamite. Few years to go yet, though."

It didn't take Rachel long to realize she could keep up with Hooper on his Monday-morning run, at least for a while, but she wouldn't be able to talk at the same time. Fortunately he wasn't far from the end of his route, and when he asked her to drop into his house for something cold to drink, she readily accepted.

Hooper's house was smaller than DeMarco's but about right for one person and even better situated for a scenic view in all directions. The living room was dominated by athletic trophies, more from his current Seniors' exploits than his original career in the thirties.

The cold drink she was offered was a highly caffeinated nondiet cola, and she couldn't help noting the contrast with the greenish health drink she'd received from the far less healthy-seeming Arthur Blemker.

Rachel felt a little odd getting down to the business at

hand in the face of Hooper's smiling hospitality, but she overcame her reluctance without much effort.

"Mr. Hooper, I've just been reading a book in which I think you're a character," she said brightly.

"Oh, really? Let's see now. That could either be an ancient track manual or one of these coffee-table books celebrating B movies."

"No, this is fiction, and you don't appear under your own name. There are plenty of similarities, though."

"Well, that's either a heck of an honor or fodder for a lawsuit. Let's hear it. Who wrote this book?"

"Wilbur DeMarco."

Jack Hooper looked puzzled. "Was Wilbur writing something about Idyllwild?"

Rachel shook her head. She briefly told him about the unfinished manuscript and the way she had identified him with the character of actor John Forbes. He listened, blank-faced, but didn't say anything. Rachel went on to recount what little she knew about the Committee for Freedom and Justice; about Wilbur's romance with Sally Jordan; and about Sally's murder in Times Square. Soon she ran out of things to say and waited for Jack Hooper to speak.

"What do you want out of all this?" he asked finally.

"I basically want to know who killed Wilbur DeMarco."

"I didn't."

"No, I don't think you did, but I think you know some things that might be helpful."

"*You're* not writing a book, are you?" he said with mild sarcasm.

"Not me. I promise. Oh, I may be able to sell this article, but if I do, it will be just a collection of general reminiscences, nothing specifically about Wilbur's death."

Hooper sighed. "Okay, I was at that New Year's Eve party, when we heard what happened to Sally.

"Sally's death was tragic because of what she represented—hope for the future, a 'new order' as we might have

168

called it. And whoever killed her was like Henry Ford's goons on the overpass, the guys that beat up Reuther and Frankensteen, trying to maintain the old order by brute force." Hooper raised his hands in the air, as though they could explain better than he could. "Okay. I said I had nothing to do with politics, but I was lying. I was involved, along with Wilbur and Sally and the others. And Rachel, even if we turn our backs on our youthful ideas, we still remember we had 'em and why we had 'em. Most of my family are dead now, but I've been concealing my brief season as a left-wing activist for so long, it's gotten to be a habit. Not much point any more, maybe, but I still wouldn't want it widely publicized. I probably wasn't much good to the Committee for Freedom and Justice. I could get very fired up about social inequities, but I was also terrified my father would find out what I was up to. Maybe it was the cloak-and-dagger aspect of it that appealed to me, though most of the members were fairly open about their involvement—we weren't Communists or anything, you know, just people who were concerned about the way things were and wanted to make them better. I'd competed with a lot of black athletes and got to know them, and I was especially fired up about lynchings down South and the Scottsboro Boys' case. We raised funds to help pay for lawyers." He smiled. "Klingsburg used to draw caricatures and sell them at our fund-raisers. What a strange guy he was. Sally Jordan was a heck of a lady. I guess we all kinda loved her, but we knew she belonged to Wilbur."

"And was there a leak in the organization's funds?"

Hooper nodded. "We all trusted each other too much. The system for accounting for money wasn't as tight as it should have been. Somebody stole us blind."

"Who?"

"No harm in saying now, I guess. I always thought it was Eric Chambers."

"Not Monte Fanning?"

Suddenly a brief anguish flashed on Hooper's face. "Oh,

169

you know about him? No, Monte wasn't guilty, the poor bastard. If he'd just been able to face things, but no, the minute a couple of members of the Committee approached him with some questions, he had to stick a .38 in his mouth, and after that, everybody really was convinced he was guilty. It's easy to pin anything on somebody who's dead, especially somebody who makes himself dead. That's no way out, but it's always been a popular escape among the movie crowd. Like my Estelle, but even she was tougher than poor old Monte." Hooper shook his head.

"Who did you say was guilty of stealing the funds?"

"Eric Chambers did it. It was Eric, no question about it."

"Wasn't he the actor who played in *Barricades* with Sally Jordan?"

"Yes, they both went back to New York for it. At that time, we knew there was a leakage but didn't know who was responsible."

"And when did you find out?"

"We never did for sure."

"Just a minute ago, you said there was no question about it. Why do you think it was Chambers?"

Hooper didn't answer for a moment, as though weighing some inner scales before deciding what to say next. Finally, he said, "I know it was Chambers. One night when we were counting the take at a labor benefit, I as good as caught him with his hand in the till."

"Why didn't you reveal what you knew?"

"Can't you guess? He blackmailed me. Said he'd reveal my involvement with the Committee to my father. I'd have been cut off without a cent, and I was smart enough to know even then I didn't have the talent to sustain even a second-rate movie career."

"Anyone in the Committee could have given you away."

"But trusting soul that I was, it never dawned on me anyone would have till Chambers threatened it. Maybe he wouldn't have done it either, but he was desperate. He gave me quite a sob story about why he needed the money. So I didn't give him away. In '38, the Committee had to disband because of the leakage of funds. We couldn't trust each other any more. Monte Fanning was the number-one suspect, and when he killed himself, he became the scapegoat. But that didn't mean we could reconstitute the Committee. We didn't want to look too close at what really happened. Certainly I didn't. I could have saved Monte, but how was I to know he'd blow his head off with a .38? Poor weak miserable bastard! I kept my mouth shut about what I knew."

"You hadn't said anything even after Sally Jordan was murdered?"

"What do you mean?"

"Didn't it ever occur to you that she could have found out what Chambers had been up to and that he might have killed her to silence her?"

"That's a ridiculous idea."

"Why?"

"Well—I don't think Chambers was a murderer. If he was he would have killed me, too. I knew his secret."

"Maybe you weren't as immediate a threat as Sally Jordan was. Maybe she really was going to reveal him, and he knew you wouldn't."

"You think I would have kept my mouth shut if I suspected that?"

"I don't know. Maybe Chambers even killed Monte Fanning. Maybe it wasn't really suicide."

Hooper shook his head. "It was suicide all right. A gun in the mouth in a locked room. In real life, that would even be enough to convince a mystery writer like Wilbur."

"What else can you tell me about Chambers?"

Hooper shrugged. "Well, that wasn't his real name."

"What was it?"

"I don't know, some German name. He'd been born in Germany, taken an English name and got rid of his accent."

"You don't think he could have been a Nazi spy, do you?"

171

Hooper smiled humorlessly. "I don't think so, no. Here's the most ironic part. Chambers was a soldier on the Allied side in World War II. He died a hero's death, left a wife and an infant daughter behind. He was probably the biggest show business name to die in actual combat during the war." Hooper spread his hands. "Well, Rachel, I've told you all I know. I don't think it has anything to do with what happened to Wilbur, or Sally either if that case is still open, and I'm trusting you not to pass any of it on needlessly."

"No, I won't. Needlessly. One more question, though."

"Yes?"

"Did you tell Wilbur all this?"

Hooper drew in a deep breath and blew it out savagely. "Yes, yes, I did. He swore he'd never give me away. Did he? I mean, how did you find out?"

Rachel shook her head. "Wilbur never gave you away. When did you tell him?"

"Just a couple of weeks before he died. With everybody else in Idyllwild, Wilbur was regarded as closemouthed, but not with me. He was always going at me about the old days. He had an obsession with what happened to Sally. I think he talked to me because he knew I'd never mention any of it to anybody else. I never intended to tell him about Chambers, but one day I finally let it slip."

"How did he react?"

"All of a sudden he was as cryptic with me as with everybody else. I could almost see the wheels kinda turning in his head. He had every right to hate me, but I had the feeling he wasn't even thinking about what a miserable fink I was. He was thinking about Monte—they were good friends, and it must have been hard on him thinking all these years that Monte had been stealing from the Committee. Now he knew it wasn't really Monte, that the guy's reputation was needlessly blackened. I think he was figuring things out, Rachel, things I don't even understand about."

"Did Wilbur still have his old Duesenberg at the time you

had this conversation, Jack?"

"I suppose he did. I don't know."

"But it was about two weeks before his death that you talked?"

Hooper considered it. "Maybe closer to three."

"It sounds like he got rid of the car after he talked to you."

Hooper shrugged. "We didn't talk about his car. I haven't seen it in months."

"Do you know that car's history?"

"No."

"Do you remember anything about Wilbur and Sally witnessing a traffic accident in 1937?"

"Wow! How the heck did you know about that? Nobody knew about that."

"Then there *was* an accident," Rachel said triumphantly.

"Oh, then you really *didn't* know about it. Not very many people could have told you. Oh, well, I might as well spill all the beans at once."

"If you knew about it, wouldn't some of the other people in your group? Klingsburg for instance?"

"I suppose he might have, but it wasn't a general topic of conversation. Besides the studio people and a few police, I always thought it was just the three of them and me that knew."

"The three of them?"

"Wilbur and Sally and Monte Fanning."

"Fanning witnessed it, too?"

"Oh, yes. And only they knew who the actress involved was. They never told me, though I had my suspicions, of course."

"What exactly do you know?"

"Late one night, they witnessed a fancy car running down a pedestrian. The pedestrian was killed, they called the police, the driver was some female star, the studio hushed it up. And the three of them cooperated with the cover-up, whether out of sympathy or what I don't know. I doubt they could have been bought off. That's all."

"And you didn't know Frances Payne was the star?"

"As I said, I had my suspicions."

"I think Wilbur's Duesenberg was involved in that accident."

"No kidding? I'll be damned."

Rachel thought she'd found out all she could from Hooper, but she had one last question. "Why did you show up at Wilbur's garage sale, Jack?"

Jack Hooper looked puzzled. "I don't know. It had something to do with facing things, I guess. Facing the past, facing the future. You know, I've been a heck of a lucky man in a lot of ways. I never really understood anything but running races. Real estate, movie acting, social activism, it was all a big mystery to me. And now here I am living comfortably in the most beautiful spot in the world and running races again, doing just what I want to do. I know all my times, year by year, but if you asked me to tell you what kind of a man I was, what I was good for, I couldn't tell you."

After her talk with Jack Hooper, Rachel took a desultory walk to the center of Idyllwild. Her head was full of theories. Fanning and Sally and Wilbur see the accident. Fanning and Sally and Wilbur all dead. Violently. Did Frances eliminate them all? But Fanning had died in a locked room, a certain suicide. And their deaths were separated by fifty years. And she had no reason to suppose Frances had an opportunity in each case anyway. She tried to take her mind off the problem, let her subconscious work. Her subconscious had always been a better detective than she had anyway.

She had a look at the posters advertising the Rustic Theater's latest double feature and glanced at the offerings in the windows of some of the realty offices. Pricing houses was always fun, even when she was only giving it half her attention. Jud Crompton swept past her, unseeing, through the door of Acorn Realty. He seemed very angry about

174

something or other, and she wondered what. Had his mysterious development scheme, or whatever it was, developed a hitch?

She walked toward the Puttering and Pans shop, tempted to stop and have a chat with Alice Zimmer. As she approached, Dorie Moss was coming out.

"Hello, Rachel. No interviews today?"

"No, not this morning. How are you, Dorie?"

"Pretty well. Been in there?" she asked, gesturing with her head toward the shop.

"Oh, yes."

"Doesn't she have a lot of dreadful merchandise?" Dorie asked in a lowered tone. "She is a pleasant young woman, though, when you get her off the dance floor. Some of the things in Wilbur's house could really bring a price in there. She admits it, too. But she'd rather sell contemporary kitsch. At least old kitsch is quaint, don't you think?" The older woman shook her head in annoyance. "Oh, listen to me rattle on. I think I owe you an apology, Rachel. Gil tells me I said too much to that sheriff's deputy and got him in trouble and you in trouble. I didn't mean to."

Rachel smiled. "You didn't get anybody in trouble, Dorie. Nothing I do is any secret."

"Well, that makes me feel better. Which way you walking?"

"Over toward Strawberry Creek, I think."

"Then I'll say goodbye. You have a good afternoon." She grasped Rachel's wrist before walking on. "You know, I think you have a better chance of finding out what happened to Wilbur than that deputy."

"That's the loyal feminist in you talking, Dorie."

"Well, maybe. 'Bye now."

When Rachel had reached the front of the post office, she saw Roger Payne standing there smiling with his day's mail in his hand.

"I'm glad I ran into you," he said.

175

"Oh?"

"I should apologize again about the other day on the trail. I guess I'm always apologizing to you, aren't I? It beats not seeing you at all."

"You could scare people that way, Roger. And you could get hurt, too. What would you have done if Stu had been carrying a gun?"

"How many people get a chance to die for love? But I'm forgetting what I wanted to tell you about. When I drove by the DeMarco house this morning, I saw a strange car in the drive and a couple of people on the deck. Do you have guests?"

"No, I don't know anything about it."

"Then you better get back there and see what's up. You on foot?"

"In Idyllwild, I'm almost always on foot."

He gestured to his spotless yellow pickup. "Can I give you a ride home, then?"

"Okay, thanks." Roger didn't seem very wolfish this morning, and she was curious about who her unannounced visitors might be.

21

When Roger Payne pulled up in front of the DeMarco house, there were two cars already parked there and three people visible on the deck. The two men Rachel recognized immediately—Gil Franklin and Arthur Blemker, Wilbur's cousin—and one of the cars was Gil's. The woman was unfamiliar, but judging from her advanced age and diminutive stature, Rachel knew who she must be.

"Want me to come in with you, Rachel?" Roger asked. All this male protectiveness could get oppressive.

"No, thanks. Gil's there, and the other man has a perfect right to be. Thanks for the ride, Roger." She got out, waved, and walked toward the house. The front door was unlocked, and she walked right in, calling "Hello!"

Arthur Blemker was the first to appear through the door that led to the deck. "Hi, Rachel," he said. "Sorry to bust in on you like this. We ought to have let you know we were coming. But the lady can be pretty persuasive."

At that moment, the lady herself came through the door. She was indeed tiny, and her gray business suit looked oddly out of place in the mountain scenery. She looked as old as either of her male companions, but her movements were quick as a hummingbird's. She exuded energy. It was not hard to imagine her dominating a room full of publishing executives, half a century ago or even now.

"Hannah Spurgeon?" Rachel ventured.

"And you're Rachel. I guess we don't need an introduction. I'm sorry to intrude on your hideaway."

"I didn't come here to hide, and I'm delighted to meet you."

"I wanted to see this place, and I twisted Arthur's arm to drive me up. When he said he wanted to set off at eight o'clock, I didn't even turn a hair, and you'd never catch me getting up at that hour in New York. I've always been a night person, you see."

"How long have you been out here?"

"Flew in yesterday. Just as soon as I could get Irvine and Campbell to spring for my ticket. We're going to make Wilbur DeMarco the detective fiction comeback of the '80s, aren't we, Arthur?"

"I guess we are if you have anything to say about it." Blemker seemed amused, and Rachel sensed he liked his cousin's old editor more than he'd expected to.

"Why don't we all sit down?" Rachel suggested.

It was then that Gil Franklin rather sheepishly entered from the deck. "Hi, Rachel. I was coming by to see you when I saw these folks, and I didn't know . . ."

"He didn't know if we were unauthorized intruders," Arthur Blemker said. "He was watching out for you."

"I appreciate that, Gil."

"Don't mention it. But now I suppose I ought to be going."

"You don't have to go, Gil. Please join us. I'll make some coffee."

"There's no need for coffee," Hannah Spurgeon said, and suddenly there was a consensus on the point. "We can't stay for long, and there's plenty to talk about. As you know by now, Rachel, I wasn't completely candid when we spoke on the phone. I *did* know what Wilbur's real-life crime was, but I didn't see any point in being specific about it. I didn't think it was important, and I thought your talk about solving a 1987 murder through stirring up the past was absurd. When I thought about it some more, it didn't seem quite so ridiculous as I'd thought, and if there *was* anything to it, it would be great publicity for any attempt to get Wilbur back in print." With an icy smile, she added, "I know that sounds callous, but in the entertainment business, of which publishing is a

178

part, you have to think in those terms. And books matter to me. I'd use any means at hand to get Wilbur back into print. Besides that, I want his killer to be punished. Gil Franklin here has been telling me a little bit about your investigations, but his information is fragmentary."

Gil looked even more uncomfortable. But Rachel didn't blame him. With her commanding personality, Hannah Spurgeon could probably get any data she desired from any person on any subject.

"I don't know who killed Wilbur DeMarco, Ms. Spurgeon," Rachel said.

"Hannah. Anything but first names seems inappropriate on the West Coast. Gil told me Charles Freeman lives up here. Freeman had every reason to hate Wilbur for taking Sally Jordan away from him, and he also was in New York at the time Sally was murdered in Times Square. I know there are other people up here who knew Wilbur in his Hollywood days. But how many would there be who also had the opportunity to be in Times Square on New Year's Eve? Have you talked to Freeman?"

"Only on the phone."

"He talked to me through a closed door," Gil said. "He's not what I'd call sociable. He never leaves his house."

"Then let's go see him. He should be easy to find," Hannah Spurgeon said.

Arthur Blemker said with a smile, "Poison ivy is easy to find, Hannah, if you want to go looking for it."

"Very clever, Arthur. Can I have that embroidered into a sampler for my kitchen?"

Rachel found the relationship between Blemker and Hannah Spurgeon amusing. Was it possible they'd only known each other for a couple of days?

Gil said, "I don't know if it would be a good idea to try to see Charles Freeman."

"Why not?" Hannah demanded.

Rachel said diplomatically, "Hannah, I've been talking to

179

a lot of, uh, senior citizens in the last few days. And you can tell something from their voices."

"Oh? What's that?"

"Their spirits, I guess, and something about the state of their health. All you people are still very active and vital. But Charles Freeman sounded tired and ill. I don't think he's been running around committing murders recently."

"You could tell that from his voice, eh? And are your analyses by voice infallible?"

"No, but your voice gave me a pretty good idea of what you'd be like."

Hannah's face glinted with humor. "Any more ideas about the murder? You seem to have been looking into it more deeply than anybody."

"Considering she's not sleuthing, just doing a magazine article," Arthur Blemker said.

"Let the girl talk, Arthur. What about it? Do you know who killed Wilbur?"

"No," Rachel confessed, "I don't. But I think it's possible, maybe even probable, it wasn't the same person who killed Sally Jordan."

"You're accepting the teenage junkie theory suddenly?"

"Not at all."

"Doesn't it seem reasonable to you Wilbur spent all these years looking for Sally's murderer—you can see how obsessed he was with it from all this fifty-year-old junk he surrounded himself with—finally solved it, confronted the killer, and got killed himself for his trouble?"

"That was *your* whole theory, Rachel," Gil Franklin reminded her.

"Almost, but not necessarily."

"Well, what do you think now?"

"If I knew, I'd tell you. It's not a question of what I know but of what I *should* know."

"Rachel," Hannah said, "you talk just like Henry Friday."

"The difference is, when he made cryptic remarks, he

knew what he was talking about. I don't begin to."

Hannah turned to Arthur Blemker and said, "Arthur, I've decided I'm staying." Seeing the surprised expression on Rachel's face, she added, "In Idyllwild, I mean. Not in this house."

"You're perfectly welcome."

"No, I wouldn't think of it. I've imposed on you enough with this unscheduled drop-in. You can get me a cabin or a motel room somewhere, can't you?"

"Sure," Blemker said. Rachel noticed Gil Franklin didn't offer his own spare room this time around. "But why?"

"I just want to see a little more of where Wilbur spent so many happy years, that's all."

When they'd left in a whirlwind, Rachel dropped to the sofa and pondered that last remark. Had Wilbur spent "so many happy years" here, or had he spent one year over and over again until he thought he had it right?"

22

THAT EVENING, RACHEL sat before the fire reading the last of the Henry Friday novels. It was *Murder Threw Friday*, the 1937 book in the series, and it was as baffling and potentially as enthralling as any of the others, but it wasn't holding her attention. She had the feeling her investigations had brought her very close to the truth about Wilbur DeMarco's death, but still she was not quite there. And now one more of the principals, if she could think of Hannah Spurgeon that way, was in residence on the hill. Not that she really considered Hannah Spurgeon a serious suspect, at least in Wilbur's murder, and she was somewhat charmed by the idea of what might be a late-budding romance between Hannah and Arthur Blemker.

A noise from outside served to distract her even more. It sounded like the cry of a child, perhaps calling for a lost pet, but it seemed to repeat itself at intervals. Gil had told her a screech owl sounded like that, and perhaps if nothing else tonight, she could add to her wildlife sightings. She went out the side door onto the deck, careful to leave it unlocked. Even with a heavy sweater on, it was a bit too cold to be outside for long. The mountain temperature dropped quickly on spring evenings. But as she turned and looked toward the road, she could see in the bright moonlight the outline of an owl sitting in one of the trees at the front of the house. Most of the owl outlines you would see here or elsewhere these days were phony ones, designed to scare away other birds, but this one was real: it proved it by turning its head to have a look at her. She was tempted to go inside for her binoculars, but she knew the owl would fly away before she could come back. Indeed any move from her now might frighten the bird off. So she stood and watched it in the moonlight, pondering how long she wanted to stand there and freeze in the interest of observing nature.

External forces made the decision for her. An explosion as sharp and deafeningly loud as anything she had ever heard assaulted her ears at the same instant a chunk of wood splintered out of the deck railing next to her. She had opened the door, flung herself through it and to the floor of the house, and closed it behind her before she intellectualized the fact that someone had just taken a shot at her.

Yes, at her. Not at the owl. Unless the hunter was a breathtakingly bad shot.

Anxious not to show any profile that might be seen through the window, Rachel reached up with a trembling hand to lock the door to the deck behind her. Was the front door locked, too? Yes, she was sure she'd left it that way, thank God.

Then a sound from the front door made the question academic. A key was turning in the lock.

To make it as hard for her assailant as she could, she reached for the cord of the 1937-vintage floorlamp she'd been reading by and yanked it out of the wall. With the violence of the act, the lamp fell over on its side. Now the only light in the room came from the fireplace, and there was little she could do about that. Fortunately the fire had come down from its earlier roaring to a mere glow.

The door opened. Over the top of the table, she could see the outline of a figure appearing in the doorway. She had nowhere to go. All she could do was not move and hope she wouldn't be seen. But she had no weapon to defend herself and couldn't stay invisible forever.

The figure walked into the room cautiously. Rachel still wasn't sure if it was a man or a woman, but she could see the outline of a gun in her visitor's right hand. After almost killing her from a distance just moments before, how could the intruder miss her at closer range?

The figure took a couple of steps forward, glancing toward the fireplace on the left, the kitchen on the right. Rachel looked for something to fling at the intruder, but there was nothing to hand on the low coffee table. The table was too heavy to lift up and use as a shield.

"Where are you, Rachel?" said a soft voice. A female voice, and Rachel thought she recognized it, though it had an unfamiliar note of menace in it now.

The woman with the gun took one more step forward, and now her face was illuminated in the light from the fireplace. Now Rachel knew for sure who her assailant was.

"Come on out, Rachel," said Alice Zimmer. "You know you can't hide from me forever."

Rachel stayed as still as she could. The fireplace crackled. Couldn't Alice hear her breathing?

Alice looked toward the kitchen to her right, peering into the shadows to see if she could spot Rachel there. Then she moved forward into the room with her back toward the kitchen.

Alice started moving around the table, peering into the semidarkness. Rachel wondered why Alice couldn't see her. Her night vision must be poor.

Suddenly Alice and not her handgun roared. She had lost her balance, tripping over the fallen floorlamp, and Rachel knew she'd better move quickly while she could. She lunged for the gun as it loosened in Alice's hand, pointed away from her. Alice fell to her knees, the gun dropping to the rug out of her reach. Rachel was still on her feet and able to dive for it. She picked it up, her back to the side door, flicked on a wall switch that lit up the whole room from the ceiling fixture. She pointed the gun with determination.

Alice's face combined frustration, fear, and calculation. "You wouldn't fire it, Rachel," she said. "You wouldn't have the nerve."

"Oh yes, I would," she said slowly. "You just try me, Alice."

As she said it, she knew it was true. She didn't want to pull the trigger, and she'd do her best to wound rather than kill, but she could shoot if she had to. And because she believed it, Alice believed it as well.

"All right. Maybe you would. I didn't really want to hurt you, Rachel."

"Is that why you took a shot at me from up on the road?"

"That was foolish. I'm a terrible shot. Jud always said so."

"But you were getting closer. Where'd you get the key to this house?"

"From Jud. What do you think? He got the listing for it from the estate. DeMarco's cousin gave him the key."

"Did you borrow the gun from Jud, too?"

"Yes, the gun, too."

"Is it the same one you used to kill Wilbur DeMarco?"

Alice sighed heavily. "Sure."

"And does Jud know about all this? Is he an accessory?"

"An accessory. That's a good word for Jud. Like a handbag or a scarf. It's about all he was good for. He should have come after you tonight, not me. I told him you were onto his real-estate scam, that you were going to give him away."

Rachel almost smiled. "But I'm not onto his real-estate scam at all. What was it?"

"Some tax thing. He was running off the hill to cook deals with some phony escrow company and their lawyers, falsifying documents. I don't really understand it."

"Did he know you killed Wilbur DeMarco?"

"No, no," she said wearily. "Jud wasn't the man I thought he was. He was a great dancer, but he had no backbone." Rachel registered the past tense Alice kept using in reference to Jud and wondered what it meant.

Alice looked up at Rachel and put some of the open friendliness back in her face as if by force of will. The effect was grotesque.

185

"Aw, Rachel, you don't have to hold any gun on me. I know it's all over with now. I didn't want to hurt you really. I just got a little crazy."

"Alice, you stay right where you are until the police get here."

"I don't remember seeing you call them," said Alice slyly.

"Well, I did."

Of course, she hadn't, and the phone wasn't within easy enough reach for her to make the call without removing her fixed attention from Alice. And she wasn't about to do that. If someone had heard the shot, maybe there would be some help on the way. In the meantime, it seemed best to keep the woman talking.

"Want to tell me about how you killed Wilbur while we wait?"

"How long have you known it was me?"

"Not long really." That was the truth. "But I think I should have known it sooner than I did."

"How?"

"That name Zimmer for one thing. The German word for room or chamber. Jack Hooper told me Eric Chambers was a German who'd changed his name and died in World War II in the American armed forces, leaving a wife and daughter behind. I knew your father died in the war, too. Eric Chambers was your father, wasn't he? And Eric Zimmer was his original name."

"That's right, but so what?"

"It gives you a connection to Wilbur DeMarco and Sally Jordan and the Committee for Freedom and Justice. Tell me this, Alice. Did you know your father embezzled those funds?"

"I don't know anything of the kind. My father was a *hero*. And Wilbur DeMarco wanted to destroy his memory. And destroy me and my mother, too. I couldn't let that happen."

"Why don't you tell me about it, Alice?"

Whether it was the result of Rachel's best effort to sound

like a radio psychologist or just an eagerness to talk, Alice decided to do just that.

"He came into the shop one day, asked me if I was Eric Chambers' daughter. Well, that was no secret, really. I'd kept the name Zimmer because it was my legal name. Then he started telling me some of the things he'd found out about that damned Committee for Freedom and Justice. My father wasn't really a member, by the way."

"He wasn't?"

"He was *not*. Not really. He was doing undercover work. My mother told me so. He worked for the FBI, infiltrating left-wing organizations. My father was a good American."

"And was stealing funds part of his undercover work?"

"Whatever he did wasn't stealing, Rachel. Anyway, I decided to do a little undercover work of my own, see just what it was Wilbur DeMarco knew—or thought he knew. I pretended to be appalled at my father's so-called crime, and at the idea it should be responsible for the suicide of De-Marco's friend, Monte Fanning. I decided to play DeMarco's ally. Then he invited me to his house the night before his garage sale."

"You took Jud's gun with you?"

"Just for protection. I never intended to use it."

"Did Jud know you had the gun?"

"It doesn't matter what Jud knew or didn't know," Alice said fiercely.

"Okay, maybe it doesn't. Tell me what happened when you came to Wilbur's that night."

For just a moment, Rachel was glad the police probably weren't on their way. If Adam Kane were in the room she doubted she would have had a chance to hear Alice's account. Police had to be so careful about confessions these days.

"Old Wilbur put on quite a show, Rachel, quite a show. How he was sure the truth about his lady love's death lay somewhere in that one year, 1937, how he got obsessed with collecting everything to do with that year, how it all paid off after fifty years, how he finally figured everything out. Oh, he thought he was so cute and clever, such a mastermind."

"And it was all centered on that mantelpiece exhibit, wasn't it? The Planter's Peanut can, the Hotel Astor key, the Criterion Theater ticket, the model Chevrolet. All pointing to Times Square, New Year's Eve, 1937."

"He said my father was there that night. That he killed Sally Jordan to keep her from revealing he'd stolen those funds. And Wilbur DeMarco seemed to think I was going to help him with his plans to spread that story and ruin my father's good name. How could he think I was going to do that? I was proud of my father, and I still am, and of my mother, too, and her position in society and all the good work she does."

"And you couldn't stand the idea of the truth being revealed. So you shot Wilbur."

"Truth? Who says it was the truth?" Alice was growing more and more agitated, more and more fanatical. "It was a lie, it had to be."

"Don't you believe your father killed Sally Jordan?"

"He couldn't have proved it. How could he prove it?"

"But don't you believe it happened?"

"My father had no reason to kill her, unless it was because of her traitorous activities, and then it was an execution, not a murder. How could I know what the FBI wanted my father to do? Sally Jordan was a goddamned traitor to everything my father stood for. If she died, she deserved to die, and Wilbur DeMarco deserved to die, and you deserve to die."

"Why did you come here tonight, Alice? What made you think I was any threat to you?" Rachel thought she knew the answer, but she wanted more than anything to keep Alice talking.

"Dorie Moss came in the shop today. Silly old woman. We were talking about the value of some of the old junk in Wilbur's house. Dorie said you had that damned exhibit on the mantel, and she described it to me. But I knew I'd removed those things the night Wilbur died, so you must have put it all back together again. And why would you do that unless you were thinking along the same lines he was?"

Rachel saw a flash of car headlights illuminating the road in front of the house. Someone had come to a stop out there. Alice didn't seem to notice.

"Then when Dorie left, Jud came along, right?"

"Right. With all the trouble I had, all he wanted to do was blubber to me about how his terribly clever tax scam turned out to be a colossal bunco job on *him*. He kept babbling about some shit from Hemet and his sonofabitchin' brother-in-law in Riverside and their so-called lawyer in Beverly Hills, and how they all took him for a ride and how Frances Payne and a bunch of other clients would be after his hide. I told you he could never keep a secret from me, didn't I? Well he told me all about it, and I started to see what I hadn't wanted to before, what a weak excuse for a man he was. He'd been worried you were suspicious about his dealings already. I poured him a few drinks and tried to convince him you were onto him, that he ought to go after you and silence you."

"Come after me with the same gun that killed Wilbur. You wanted to frame him for two murders, didn't you? It never could have worked, Alice."

"Think I don't know that?"

"How much did Jud know about what you were doing?"

"I told you before, it doesn't matter what Jud knew or didn't know."

"Why doesn't it?"

"He's dead, that's why. I killed him. Tonight. He was a sniveling coward."

As Alice spoke, the door behind her opened almost silently, but a gust of cold air made her turn around. Adam Kane was standing there, gun drawn.

"He may be a coward, Ms. Zimmer," Kane said, "but I'm afraid he's a live one, and he's talking plenty."

189

23

ON TUESDAY MORNING, Adam Kane made one more visit to Wilbur DeMarco's house. Rachel invited him into the dining area, where Arthur Blemker and Hannah Spurgeon were finishing breakfast and enjoying the view. Kane declined the offer of a fried egg but accepted a cup of coffee.

"The gun that killed DeMarco and wounded Jud Crompton was his own gun all right. A .38 Colt Cobra. He didn't have a permit for it and says he just acquired it for protection."

"The same reason Alice brought it here the first time," Rachel said.

"So she says. According to Crompton, he had no idea his gun had killed DeMarco or that Alice Zimmer had 'borrowed' it that night. Insists he would have told us if he'd suspected anything, all-around good citizen that he is."

"Was Crompton badly wounded?"

"He ought to have been killed, and I can see why Alice Zimmer thought he was. It was a shot through the chest that seems to have missed everything important. He's a lucky guy."

"What did he say about Alice shooting him?"

"He said she went crazy. Wanted him to come after you, keep you from revealing what you knew about his real-estate scam. He said that was all over anyway, and he didn't want to kill anybody. She erupted. Said he was a coward, not half the man her father was, all kinds of stuff. Crompton said he didn't know what the hell she was talking about. She took the gun and shot him. He lost consciousness for a moment.

190

When people heard the shot coming from the Puttering and Pans shop, they called us. And by the time we got to Jud, he was conscious and ready to talk plenty, all the way down to the emergency room in Hemet.

"And that's how you knew Alice had come after me?"

"Right. But you didn't seem to need much help from me. You seemed to be doing just fine."

"Did you get a confession from her you can use?"

"She was ready to talk, and we were real careful to read her her rights. If she gets off at all, it'll be on mental grounds. Alice Zimmer is not real well balanced. Last thing she said was what a great dancing partner Crompton was, and how sorry she is to lose him."

Hannah Spurgeon cleared her throat. "Pardon me, but I feel like I just walked in on the middle of a movie and can't get the plot straight. Don't you, Arthur?"

Blemker said, "I have to agree. Can one of you explain the whole story from the beginning?"

"Ms. Hennings is better on the beginning than I am," Kane said. "Go ahead, and I'll just throw in my two cents worth where necessary."

Rachel smiled. "I'll probably need more than two cents worth, but here goes. Naturally, it starts in 1937, with the Committee for Freedom and Justice, the liberal political action organization Wilbur and Sally Jordan belonged to. There was a mysterious leakage of funds, and no one was sure exactly where the money was going. Actually, one person did know besides the person who was doing it, but he didn't tell anyone for reasons of his own. Late in the year, after Sally had gone east to be in the play *Barricades* on Broadway, she must have discovered that her costar, Eric Chambers, who'd also been a member of the Committee group in Hollywood, was the source of the leak. How she found out we'll never know, but I think she confronted him with the information in the early hours of New Year's Day, 1938, right in the middle of the crowd celebrating in Times

191

Square. It may have been only a few minutes after she'd talked to Wilbur on the phone back in Hollywood. Chambers stabbed her to death. In the crowd, no one was able to identify him, and he got away with it.

"The death of Sally Jordan almost destroyed Wilbur. The activities that had meant something to him—writing screenplays and detective novels, being active in liberal political activities—suddenly meant nothing. Being haunted by her death was what led him to his obsession with 1937 and this collection he gathered.

"For a while, Wilbur continued at least trying to continue his writing career. When he wrote to you in January of '38, Hannah, he still intended to fulfill his contract."

Hannah nodded. "Yes, and I thought he would. But I think something else happened. I never knew what."

"I think it was his friend Monte Fanning's suicide in March 1938 that derailed his career for good. Fanning was the scapegoat for the missing funds, and Wilbur must have found his culpability hard to believe, but the suicide made it appear to be true. And Fanning had died in a locked room, a real taunt of fate as far as Wilbur was concerned. I can imagine Wilbur telling himself, in a book this would be murder, but in life, it's nothing but a messy suicide. The world of Henry Friday became remoter to him, and maybe more absurd and futile, than ever.

"We have to remember that Wilbur didn't connect the shortages in the Committee for Freedom and Justice coffers with Sally's death, especially after Fanning's suicide seemed to clear that up. I think his prime suspect was Charles Freeman, a man he'd never met, who was Sally's husband. Freeman was giving Sally a divorce, but Wilbur might have thought Freeman was the sort of man who could kill her rather than give her up to another man. Getting closer to Freeman was probably the reason he first moved to Idyllwild, though there were other acquaintances from his Hollywood days up here, notably William Klingsburg, the muralist, and

192

Jack Hooper, the Olympian turned actor.

"And there was another theory he obviously explored, at considerable expense. Early in 1937, he and Sally and Monte Fanning witnessed the traffic accident that precipitated Frances Payne's spell in a mental institution. He thought she might have killed Sally, fearing exposure. He acquired her old Duesenberg and began driving it around town. That was about the same time Frances went into permanent seclusion. Whether the one thing caused the other Wilbur didn't know, but anyway it didn't solve his case. I played with that theory quite a bit myself, even considering the possibility that Monte Fanning actually was murdered in his locked room. But when I thought about it, I realized Wilbur had abandoned the theory and gotten rid of the car as soon as he learned the truth about the missing funds from Jack Hooper. He got rid of the car two weeks before his death, clear enough evidence that he got rid of the theory at the same time.

"I don't know exactly what course Wilbur's investigations took up here. Maybe he talked to Klingsburg and Freeman about his quest. Freeman denied ever meeting him, but Klingsburg didn't, and it seems Wilbur would have at least tried to talk to them. Certainly he talked to Jack Hooper, and that was how he finally found out Eric Chambers had been guilty of the embezzlement, and that was what led him to the next step in his reasoning. When he was able to make the connection between Chambers and the embezzlement, he formed the theory that Chambers might have killed Sally. With the killer dead, it would have been a rather unsatisfactory ending to his quest. But it caused his enthusiasm for collecting 1937 to vanish. He made the same deduction I did about Alice Zimmer's last name—or maybe he already knew the truth.

"Chambers may or may not have told his wife about the embezzlement, and she possibly at least suspected he had been involved in the death of Sally Jordan. If she did, I'm sure she never told her daughter, who knew her father only as a war hero. Oh, and her mother also gave Alice a story that Eric Chambers was some kind of government agent, infiltrating left-wing organizations."

"I'm pretty sure that was just her mother's fantasy," said Adam Kane. "To protect her from the truth."

"Anyway, Wilbur invited Alice here the night of his death to show her his mantelpiece exhibit and explain his theory about Sally Jordan's death. From Alice's description, he must have presented his account of what happened in a very dramatic way, just as an old-time mystery writer might. When Stu and I met Wilbur the day before his death, he was acting in a cryptic manner, as if he had something up his sleeve. And he said something about still being a mystery writer but not intending his future efforts for print. I think he was thinking about his meeting with Alice and the detective-story nature of his little exhibit. Wilbur's adrenaline must have been flowing by this time, but I'm sure he only wanted information from Alice. He didn't intend to be any kind of threat to her, and indeed didn't have anything against her personally. Maybe he even thought she might be an ally in his investigations. Of course, she wasn't. Alice, proud of her father's stature as a World War II hero and of her mother's social position, couldn't stand the idea of the truth being revealed, and she killed him."

"Not to change the subject, but just what was this real-estate scam of Crompton's?" Arthur Blemker asked.

Rachel smiled slightly at Adam Kane. "I think I know the answer to that one, too."

Kane gestured her to go ahead.

"I think Jud was working in concert with somebody in the escrow business to falsify documents on various sales of property, fixing the dates so that the transactions appeared to take place before the first of 1987 and could be taxed as capital gains at a lower rate under the old 1986 tax law. Do that in enough volume and you could turn a hefty profit for

194

your clients—and yourself."

"That's what Crompton *thought* he was doing all right. But how did you figure it out?"

"Roger Payne told me his mother, after making a deal with Crompton on her Meditation Point property, said she had actually made it months before. That sounded like the deal involved playing around with dates. But it was a crazy scam that could never have worked. For one thing, you'd have to have another accomplice in the County Recorder's office."

Kane nodded. "Damn right it couldn't have worked. He should have known better. It was really a con game by some guy who worked for an escrow company—or pretended to. Kind of nice to see a con man get conned himself, and I can't say I feel too sorry for any of the clients that were involved. You *can* cheat an honest man, but there weren't any honest men, or women, being cheated in this case. You should have heard Crompton spouting about how he was down at 'that so-called office in Hemet this morning and called their so-called phone number in Riverside,' and found out they'd flown the coop with front money from six or seven people on the hill, plus some of his own. He said it was like a damn pigeon drop dressed up in new clothes and now he'd have that crazy Frances Payne and the rest of those people on his back."

Adam Kane stood up. "Well, I better go. Just thought I owed you a report."

When Rachel returned to the table after showing Kane to the door, Arthur and Hannah were discussing the possibility of donating Wilbur's 1937 collection intact to a museum, if they could find the proper recipient. Rachel liked the idea and decided not to press her claim for the 1937 books. It would be a shame to separate them from the rest of the collection.

Barely a moment had passed when there was another knock on the door. She opened it, and there stood Gil Franklin, a stocky, broadly grinning septuagenarian at his side.

"Morning, Rachel. I wasn't sure if you wanted any company this morning, but Hank here insisted on coming just in case."

"Hank—?" she said.

"Sure. I've still got you booked solid for the rest of the week you know. This is your Tuesday morning appointment."

It was Wednesday evening of the following week, and Rachel was looking forward to the traditional pizza. She was shelving a few books while she waited for Stu's arrival.

He turned up promptly, holding a large, square, flat box in front of him and a promising-looking cylindrical paper bag under his arm. There being no customers in the shop, she planted a quick kiss on his cheek and turned the sign in the door to closed.

Uncharacteristically, instead of charging up the stairs with their dinner, Stu looked at the area of shelves where she'd been working, the mystery section. "Look at all these Wilbur DeMarco titles," he said, "and in terrific shape, too."

"Hannah Spurgeon sent them to me. She said she'd found them in some dusty corner of the Irvine and Campbell warehouse, and she was offering them as a gift of gratitude from the firm."

Stu set the pizza box on a bookshop ladder and pulled off one of the books, opening it to the flyleaf. "It's signed. Are they all like that?"

Rachel nodded.

Stu looked at her suspiciously. "They had all these signed copies sitting in their warehouse? How can you explain that?"

"I don't understand the publishing business. Let's eat."

If you have enjoyed this book and would like to receive details of other Walker mystery titles, please write to:

Mystery Editor
Walker and Company
720 Fifth Avenue
New York, NY 10019